LOVE INSPIRED

INSPIRATIONAL ROMANCE

D0052990

Killer Harvest

TANYA STOWE

LOVE INSPIRED SUSPENSE

INSPIRATIONAL ROMANCE

Courage. Danger. Faith.

*Find strength and determination in stories
of faith and love in the face of danger.*

AVAILABLE THIS MONTH

FUGITIVE TRAIL
ELIZABETH
GODDARD

MOUNTAIN CAPTIVE
SHARON DUNN

FALSELY ACCUSED
SHIRLEE MCCOY

STOLEN SECRETS
SHERRI
SHACKELFORD

AMISH COUNTRY
MURDER
MARY ALFORD

KILLER HARVEST
TANYA STOWE

ISBN-13: 978-1-335-40271-4

EAN

"Jared, what's going on? What are you not telling me?"

Jared turned, and the look in his eyes frightened Sassa.

"What is it? What's wrong?"

"Heiser's dead, but they're still using his tactic. Distract and attack. They're sacrificing their own people again. That leaves us spread out with our forces divided." He paused and looked her straight in the eye. "We have to get out of here. The Black Knights are coming for you."

Sassa's blood pounded through her temples. Jared ran across the room and picked up the radio.

"Lucero? Come in, Lucero. We've got to get Sassa out of here."

The radio crackled. "I just got a report of activity on the—"

The radio went silent. All the lights in the house flashed then went dark. The only sound was the refrigerator cycling down as the power went off completely.

Flickering fire from the fireplace lit Jared's features as he stared at her across the room. Sassa gripped Keri and rose to her feet.

"Jared..."

But her whisper died as muffled shots sliced the air.

Tanya Stowe is a Christian fiction author with an unexpected edge. She is married to the love of her life, her high school sweetheart. They have four children and twenty-one grandchildren, a true adventure. She fills her books with the unusual—mysteries and exotic travel, even a murder or two. No matter where Tanya takes you—on a trip to foreign lands or a suspenseful journey packed with danger—be prepared for the extraordinary.

Books by Tanya Stowe

Love Inspired Suspense

Mojave Rescue
Fatal Memories
Killer Harvest

KILLER HARVEST

TANYA STOWE

LOVE INSPIRED SUSPENSE
INSPIRATIONAL ROMANCE

LOVE INSPIRED® SUSPENSE
INSPIRATIONAL ROMANCE

ISBN-13: 978-1-335-40271-4

Recycling programs
for this product may
not exist in your area.

Killer Harvest

This edition published by arrangement with Harlequin Books S.A.

For questions and comments about the quality of this book,
please contact us at CustomerService@Harlequin.com.

Love Inspired
22 Adelaide St. West, 40th Floor
Toronto, Ontario M5H 4E3, Canada
www.Harlequin.com

Printed in U.S.A.

For I know the thoughts that I think toward you...
thoughts of peace, and not of evil,
to give you an unexpected end.
–Jeremiah 29:11

For my grandson Kaden, for reasons he will understand.

ONE

Something was wrong. Terribly wrong.

Sassa Nilsson stopped in her tracks as her mentor, supervisor and close friend, Dr. Sam Kruger, slowed his pace. All she wanted was to grab their car from the San Francisco airport parking lot and head home to her baby. Instead, Sam halted…again. He pushed his glasses on top of his gray head and stared off into the distance— a nervous habit Sassa knew quite well.

She dragged her suitcase around him then stopped and looked back. "For someone anxious to get home, you are stalling."

He nodded as if jarred from a serious thought. "Stalling…yes. Yes, I am." He pulled his glasses down, straightened his spine and headed toward the elevators.

This "trip of a lifetime" had turned into a nightmare. Sassa had been Sam's assistant for almost five years but she'd never attended even a local meeting with him. Life always seemed to get in the way. The international conference in China with the world's leading plant biologists and agriculture experts was supposed to be a dream come true. But soon after they'd arrived, Sam received a phone call. His wife, June, was ill…so ill that his incredible focus was shot to pieces. Sassa had not seen him this disturbed since he'd received word last year that his son, Christopher, had been killed in Afghanistan. That loss had almost destroyed Sam. He might not have recovered if Sassa hadn't had her baby.

Keri's birth six months ago had put joy and meaning back into Sam's life…as well as Sassa's. This trip was her first away from the baby for any length of time and it was supposed to be a crowning achievement… for both of them since she helped put together Sam's presentation. Instead she'd watched in horror as Sam bumbled through his lecture on plant viruses and bioterrorism—meant to be the highlight of the conference. He'd managed to pull it together and make his point of how easily a plant virus could wipe out the world's crops and food sources, but he hadn't come across as the expert he was. He was brilliant, even gifted, which was why, as a professor at the relatively midsize California State University at Fresno, he'd still been awarded a massive grant to study plant pathogens.

Sassa knew Sam too well. Either June was gravely ill or something else was seriously wrong.

The elevator doors opened to an almost empty luggage area. With dawn just peeking over the horizon, crowds were light. Sassa and the professor were among the first of the flight passengers to arrive at the luggage carousel. Sam's nervous gaze bounced around the empty baggage area as if searching for something. At last the machine clicked on and the carousel began to spin around.

"Sassa." Sam took her arm. "My dear, I might not be driving home with you."

"What?" Sassa spun. "You've been desperate to get home and see June. What do you mean?"

"A young man is coming to meet me. His name is Jared De Luca. He's a friend. It's just…he'll probably be in uniform. A border patrol uniform."

Sassa stared at him. "Sam, what is going on? What's wrong?"

He shook his head. "It's best you know nothing. I want to protect you and precious Keri."

"Protect us from what? You're scaring me, Sam. Tell me what's going on. Is June really ill?"

"No. I'm not sure where June is. I haven't been able to reach her since we left."

"What?"

She stared at her mentor. June was missing? Sam was afraid for Sassa and the baby? He stumbled over his words, searching for a way to explain.

Over his shoulder, Sassa spotted a man walking toward them. Was this Sam's Jared? He wasn't wearing a uniform. He wore a black leather jacket, black pants and sunglasses, even though the sun had barely risen. He looked odd. Something about his hair…it looked fake. Even his skin appeared almost waxen as he marched toward them relentlessly, like a robot.

A walking, live robot. Like the terminator from the movie.

Sam noticed her distraction and turned. He gasped and stepped toward the stranger.

"No…"

Without hesitation, the robotic newcomer pulled a knife from beneath his leather jacket, lunged and stabbed the older man. Sassa stood frozen as Sam cried out and bent over into the man's leather-clad arms. The terminator man pulled his knife from Sam's chest. As the professor sagged to the ground, the guy grabbed the strap of Sam's laptop bag, cut it free of his shoulder and spun, marching for the sliding-glass doors of the exit. Sassa watched the whole scene, frozen and speechless. She wasn't able to make a sound until Sam hit the floor.

She screamed his name and dropped beside him. Blood flowed from her friend's chest and bubbled from his mouth. Sassa cried out again, knowing Sam was mortally wounded.

"Call 9-1-1!" she screamed at the other passengers moving toward them. "Someone call for help!"

Sam struggled to speak to her.

"Don't talk, Sam. Help is on the way."

He shoved his wrist at her, the one holding his ID bracelet.

She bent over him. "Please don't move." Tears fell onto his wrist and the bracelet, tears she didn't even know she was shedding.

Sam shook his head again and tried to form a word. She leaned forward to hear him whisper, "Yours."

Then his head fell back against the cement floor with a jarring thud.

Jared De Luca stood in a corner of the interrogation room while FBI Special Investigator Daniel Kopack put Sassa Nilsson through the ringer. Jared kept his promise to remain silent, but crossed his arms tightly to hold in his frustration. He was fortunate they'd even let him in the room. Speaking up would get him tossed out.

All the while his mind ran through one refrain: if only… If only he'd convinced his superiors at the border patrol to take the threats against Dr. Kruger seriously when he'd contacted Jared a year ago. If only he hadn't taken leave, been away from his office when Sam had tried to reach him during the China trip. Sam and Sassa were three days into the conference before Jared learned that June Kruger was missing.

If only there hadn't been a struggle over jurisdiction before anyone had taken action. Was it the border patrol, the FBI or Homeland Security's job to investigate Sam's claims? Well, now that he'd been murdered, the job obviously fell under the FBI's rule and the capable hands of Agent Kopack. In spite of all Jared's words to the contrary, the man continued to assume Sassa knew about Sam's involvement with the Black Knights.

She didn't. Over the months and the multiple phone conversations he and Sam had shared, the good doctor had assured Jared time and again that Sassa knew nothing. Absolutely nothing. Sam couldn't keep the fact that he was being harassed by the environmental terrorist group from his wife, but he'd done everything he could to keep Sassa and her "precious Keri" safe. Sam had always referred to Sassa's baby as "precious Keri."

Sam had also stated that Sassa should have been called Sassy instead. She had spark and fire. She wouldn't have sat by silently, waiting for the Black Knights to act. Those were the instructions issued to Sam by Jared's superiors. The doctor had assured Jared that Sassa would have made something happen. Another reason he'd kept the information from her. He didn't want her getting into trouble with the authorities. All to no purpose.

Now she was right in the middle of this disaster and definitely didn't look sassy.

Her round face seemed hollowed out. Dark circles,

leftovers from a twelve-hour flight, rimmed her eyes. Tears had washed all her mascara into smudges beneath. Add to all that a red nose, puffy lips and long blond hair tied in a messy knot on top. The woman was bedraggled, exhausted and in shock. She didn't deserve what Kopack was putting her through and it was all Jared could do to keep silent. He couldn't give them a reason to kick him out.

The entire situation was beyond frustrating. Not to mention the fact that Kopack asked all the wrong questions. No wonder Sassa appeared to have mentally checked out.

In her hand, she clutched an ID bracelet. Sam's, of course. He'd seen it on the man's wrist many times during their phone/video chats. When had Sassa unhooked it from her boss's wrist? Why was she clutching it so tightly her knuckles turned white and her fingers red? Those were the important questions, not the accusatory ones Kopack kept throwing at her.

The agent leaned back in his chair. His self-assured manner grated Jared's nerves. He stared at Sassa for a long time before leaning forward. "What do you know about the Black Knights?"

For the first time life came into Sassa's blue eyes. She studied Kopack awhile before she drew her tongue over chapped lips. "I know they're not what they say they are."

"How's that?"

Now a real spark came into her gaze. "They say they're an environmental group, concerned with the future of the planet. But they're really environmental terrorists."

Kopack nodded. "What connection did Dr. Kruger have with the Black Knights?"

Another spark flashed in that blue gaze. Sassy Sassa had finally showed up but Jared feared her timing was all wrong. "He contacted them with questions about their organization, but he had no long-term connection with them."

"I beg to differ. We have emails. He exchanged emails with the group's leader for several months."

She nodded. "He did, a long time ago. Right after his son died in Afghanistan. Sam went through a rough patch. He was angry at the government…at the world. He wanted to do something, be part of a change. But as soon as he discovered the group's real goals, he broke contact with them."

"Not true. We have emails from two months ago."

"They were harassing him. He promised me he'd report them. Surely you know that."

Kopack shrugged. "They wanted the formula."

Sassa's lips parted and her gaze widened even more. Smart girl. She caught on faster than most. Sam had said she was one of his brightest students.

"There is no formula." Her tone hardened like bronzed steel.

"Are you sure?"

She nodded again. "Yes, I'm sure. I helped Sam destroy all our notes and information after the accident. We were working in a closed container. Sam was so cautious—he always insisted on closed containers. We had a strain of Xylella Fastidiosa and he was attempting to apply another strain of staph—" She halted and shook her head. "It doesn't matter. Our equipment failed. The arm broke, dropped a large quantity of one strain onto the virus plate then the arm fell to the bottom of the container. Sam sealed off the arm, then went back to sterilize the plate. The virus had multiplied so fast you could see it with the naked eye. It scared us."

"Why?"

Kopack was playing dumb. He knew exactly why.

Sassa's sigh sounded frustrated. "It was a pathogen. A virus that kills plants. It had multiplied with nothing to feed on." Kopack's blank look frustrated her more. "Don't you understand? The virus was growing, even without a host or a carrier. That meant it could attach to any plant, any crop and destroy it in hours or days. Airborne, it could travel the world and kill every living plant in its path. Sam tried to eradicate it. Nothing worked. Finally, he was forced to fry the equipment, everything in the container, with a blowtorch. It frightened him so much, he ordered me to wipe out all of our files so it couldn't be repeated. We hadn't recorded much, but I personally wiped most of what was there off the computer systems in the lab."

She leveled her gaze on Kopack. "I know there's no formula because it was an accident. We couldn't repeat it because we shredded what info we wrote down and what was online, we deleted. I did it myself."

Kopack shook his head. "Oh, there's a formula… and the Black Knights knew your mentor had found it. That's what they were after when they killed him. They stole his computer bag. Didn't you wonder why, Ms. Nilsson? By the way, what is your real name? Up until a year ago you were known as Sassa Larsen."

Her jaw stiffened and Jared winced.

Don't lose your cool now, Sassa. Don't you see he's baiting you?

"I'm divorced. I preferred to go back to my maiden name."

"Where is Mr. Larsen?"

"I haven't a clue. Probably at the closest casino. He's not my problem anymore."

"On the contrary, he might be your biggest problem. As you noted, your ex is always looking for money. Is it possible he offered to get the formula for the Black Knights for a price?"

Her lips parted. "I haven't seen Erik in over a year. He has yet to lay eyes on his own daughter."

"Then how did the Black Knights discover the formula?"

She closed her eyes. "There…is…no…formula."

Slowly, Kopack turned in his seat and leveled his gaze on Jared.

"What do you say, Officer De Luca? Is there a formula?"

Thanks, man. Way to put me on the spot.

Jared sighed, hooked his thumbs on his gun belt and met Sassa's wide-eyed stare. "Yes. There is."

Sassa stared at the tall stranger in the corner. Black hair, slightly wavy. High cheekbones and dark eyes. A chin that looked carved from granite and a perfectly trimmed goatee with a little five-o'clock shadow behind it. Maybe he'd had a rough night, too, as rough as hers. But those wide shoulders looked like they could handle anything that came his way, and he was handsome. Too handsome. She'd learned all about handsome men and their oh-so-charming ways from her ex.

"Excuse me. Exactly who are *you*?" The *you* came out with all the scorn she had for his type and her gaze scoured down the green uniform to the gun belt wrapped around his waist.

Green uniform. "Wait…are you Sam's young man? The border patrol agent he was watching for?"

"Yes, I am."

She was exhausted, worn to a frazzle, and now she was angry. Ready to lash out.

"You were late…too late."

He winced as if in pain.

Good. At least one of these cold, brusque men with their blank faces had the decency to feel something for Sam…kind, gentle Sam. Tears pricked her eyes and she looked down, refusing to cry again, especially in front of the man who had failed Sam in so many ways.

"You're the 'official' he contacted regarding the Black Knights. You've been talking to him since all this started. Why didn't you stop that man from killing him? And why on earth did he contact the border patrol in the first place?"

That verbal dart seemed to strike a chord. He straightened his broad shoulders. "I head up the border patrol's bio-terrorism section in Riverside. Sam and I had a previous connection regarding a species of plant coming in from Mexico. I'm a biologist. He knew I'd understand the pathogen's danger."

His words didn't mollify Sassa. Sam was dead. No amount of credentials, connections or degrees would change that. Besides…

"There is no formula." She grated it out, determined to make her point.

"Yes, there is, Sassa. You were right. The pathogen's potential terrified Sam. He wanted to develop a cure. We provided him with the equipment to work from a secret lab in his home."

Sassa wanted to snipe and argue, but what he said

struck deep. His words made sense and rang with truth. Sam had been distracted, preoccupied for months, like he behaved when working on a project. She'd thought he was spending more time with his wife. June deserved the attention, so Sassa never questioned the time off or the extra hours.

A thought hit her like a blow. "He had no resources. He had to access the internet. These people could have hacked the computer in his home and discovered he was working on a formula."

De Luca shook his head. "He wasn't hacked. We supplied him with a private server connected directly to ours. He had the best computer protection our government could provide. And…he wasn't working on the formula. He completed it."

"The virus is real. And now they have it," she whispered. Cold swept over her, so deep and chilling, her hands trembled.

"How…how could you let this happen?" Her tone was harsh. The dam holding her emotions in check had burst. "Why didn't you stop him from developing it? Why weren't you on time?"

Her words seemed to reach their target. De Luca winced as if she'd actually struck him.

"Don't be so hard on Officer De Luca, Ms. Nilsson." She turned toward the lead agent, ready to lash out at him, too. "The Black Knights created a very complicated diversion—a bomb scare in the airport precisely at the right moment. Besides, we didn't leave Dr. Kruger unprotected. We had a man following you both throughout the trip. We found his body in a bathroom stall on the upper floor, not far from where you exited the plane."

Sassa stared at Kopack. The hot flames inside her died out. A man had been following them, watching them everywhere they'd gone on the trip, and she had no clue? She should have known. Should have been more aware, more cautious. Paid more attention to Sam. Instead she'd been focused on herself, her own problems and her ambition to gain a name for herself at the conference.

And she had the audacity to blame De Luca for his faults. The heat of shame tinged her cheeks. *She'd* failed Sam. The truth swamped her and threatened to drown her. A familiar sinking feeling trickled through her but she fought it. She might have failed Sam in his last days, but she wouldn't fail him in his death. She'd make the people responsible pay. Her mind kicked into overdrive.

"These so-called Black Knights… They seem to be everywhere. Know everything."

Kopack agreed and opened a file. "They are one of the most technically competent terrorist groups out there. All thanks to their leader, Nikolai Chekhov." He pulled a photo out of the file and handed it to her. "Do you recognize him?"

She studied the man in the photo and noted the waxy complexion. "Yes, he looks like the man who stabbed Sam. I recognize the strange appearance of his skin. But he had black hair."

"He was wearing a wig. We found it on the ground in the parking lot."

"He can't hide that skin. It looks half dead."

"That's because it is. Chekhov's parents were brilliant nuclear physicists working at Chernobyl. His family survived the accident and immigrated to the US. In the subsequent years, Chekhov watched his parents and his older sister die from different forms of cancer, all due to radiation exposure. Chekhov didn't escape their fate. He has severe nerve damage. It's killing him, too, but at a much slower rate."

"He wants vengeance."

"Yes, and he's very good at getting what he wants. Five years ago he joined the rather benign Knights and slowly but surely began to recruit brilliant sociopaths like himself. Eventually they took over the group and changed the name to the Black Knights, with a different goal. They don't want to protect the environment but to destroy mankind's destructive technological progress."

Sassa pressed a hand to her forehead. In spite of her determination, her overworked mind was beginning to spin. "But they neglected to change their web page and include that little piece of information. That's why Sam thought they were safe."

"Chekhov believed he'd found another conversion with Dr. Kruger. He wasn't happy when he found out he was wrong about the good doctor's intentions…and Chekhov doesn't like to be wrong. He sent his right-hand man to watch over the professor."

He pulled out another photo and handed it to her. "My people spotted him on security film in and around the campus."

Sassa stared at the agent, unable to move. At last, she looked at the picture of a stocky man with a long black beard and a ponytail. She had to work hard to get her eyes to focus. Finally, her blurred vision cleared. She closed her eyes, dropped her forehead to her hand and shook her head. "I don't recognize him. I don't think I've ever seen him. Sam developed the formula and I didn't know… Men have been watching us on campus and following us…around the world, and I'm clueless. I'm sorry, Agent Kopack, but I'm useless to you."

She was no longer able to fight the familiar feeling of failure, and it moved over her in a wave that dragged her body down. Tears came again. She couldn't stop them this time and didn't try. She covered her eyes with one hand and let them fall. "I just want to go home and hold my baby."

After a short pause, Kopack cleared his throat. "I think we're finished for now. Let's—"

"Hold on." Officer De Luca interrupted whatever Kopack meant to say. "You said Sam told you his ID bracelet was yours."

Surprised, Sassa wiped the tears from her cheeks, sat up and opened her hand. She'd forgotten Sam's gift. She'd clutched it so tightly during this interrogation that deep imprints grooved her skin. In fact, a small, slightly bloody spot showed where the latch had pierced the inside of her palm.

"May I see it?"

Officer De Luca's request jarred her. Numb, she handed it to him with a jerky motion.

He ran his fingers across the numbers engraved on the face of the ID plate. "These numbers look like they could be a code of some sort, or maybe a combination."

Sassa shook her head and lowered her forehead back onto her hand. "No. It's nothing like that. Sam's grandfather was a pastor in Germany during World War Two. Like many other Christian leaders, he protested the treatment of the disabled and the mentally ill so loudly, he ended up in a concentration camp. That's the number assigned to him. Sam was very proud of his grandfather's actions. He put the number on that bracelet to honor him. He meant to give it to Christopher. After his son died, Sam told me he wanted me to have it. It has nothing to do with the formula. I'm sorry. Like I said, I'm no help."

She looked up and tried to focus on Agent Kopack. "Can I go home now?"

The agent nodded. "Yes. We've arranged for transportation. You're in no shape to make the three-hour drive back to Fresno."

She sighed with relief. "Kingsburg. My home is in Kingsburg."

Now Kopack looked blank.

"It's a small town a short drive out of Fresno." Officer De Luca supplied the information. "I'll take her there."

"My agents are perfectly capable—"

"I'm taking her." De Luca's tone allowed for no arguments. He came around to her side of the table and assisted Sassa from her chair. She wasn't certain she wanted him to make sure she got home safely but the grip on her arm was steady. In fact, his big, broad-shouldered body seemed to be the only thing holding her up. Her legs refused to work. She leaned on him as he half carried her out the door.

"My bag and my luggage."

"I've got it, Sassa. Don't worry."

Don't worry? If only.

Jared glanced at Sassa in the passenger seat next to him. The minute they'd climbed into his government-issued SUV, she'd pushed the seat back and fallen asleep. Three agents followed behind them; two in her car and another in a government car. Two of the agents would stay to guard Sassa at her parents' house near Kingsburg. As soon as they dropped her off, Jared and the other agent would return to the small office in downtown Fresno.

They'd set up a temporary office four days ago when Sam had notified him that June was missing. The FBI had mobilized and was on site quickly. He'd been impressed. The same day he'd returned from Los Angeles and retrieved Sam's message, they had him traveling to Fresno. Still, it hadn't been fast enough to save his friend.

Jared stumbled over the thought of Sam's death. The Black Knights had moved like lightning. After months of no activity and no contact with Sam, they'd snatched June off the street and attempted to blackmail Sam into handing over the formula. If the Black Knights couldn't force Sam to hand over the formula, they had a "Plan B" to steal it.

Whirlwind fast. Jared would never underestimate them again—or rather, he'd never underestimate Nikolai Chekhov. He was the mastermind. A brilliant sociopath. Sassa had called him the Terminator, the robot-like creature from the movie of the same name. She'd referred to the unusual look of his skin and the emotionless features, all caused by the nerve damage that was killing him. But his mind, his brilliant mental capacity, was as robotic as his physical features. Like a computer, the man seemed ten steps ahead of the authorities. At least, he had been so far. They would have to scramble to get ahead. That was Jared's sole purpose now. He would think further ahead, move quicker and never underestimate Chekhov. He wouldn't fail again.

Sassa stirred and groaned. He glanced over. Her

neck was in an awkward, twisted position. She groaned again, quiet and soft. A nice sound. Kind of personal. He liked it. In fact, now that he'd finally met Sassa, he'd discovered he liked a lot of things about her.

She was bright. Jared should have realized that. Sam wouldn't have chosen an assistant who wasn't extremely capable. In the interrogation, Kopack had intentionally left out information. Sassa had put the pieces together with skill. Sam's murder had devastated her. That was obvious. But she hadn't let emotion control her. She'd responded with a calm balance most people could not have summoned.

Those capabilities, combined with some nice features—eyebrows with little pointed peaks and bow-shaped lips—made it look as if she was always on the verge of a smile. Her appearance exuded likability. Usually, he didn't go for curvy women. He preferred them tall and slender like Jessica…

Thinking of his wife—ex-wife now—was not a good idea. That whole situation had sent him into a tailspin and caused this disaster. If Jared hadn't been forced to attend his divorce court date in LA, he might have received Sam's call. He'd have been able to alert the authorities earlier and his friend might be alive today.

Jared's jaw tightened. Now he could add that to his list of mistakes. He'd spent the last year of his separation from Jessica going over what he'd done wrong, wondering how he might have changed things to make his marriage work. He still didn't have the answers and hanging on to a dead marriage had only made him seem pitiful in Jessica's eyes. She didn't understand how or why making it work mattered so much to him.

Sometimes he didn't understand himself.

Maybe it had something to do with his grandfather and his Christian values...values Jared wasn't sure he shared anymore. He'd lost faith in a God that didn't seem to care. He'd learned that early in life with his alcoholic mother. But he'd been so busy trying to prove himself worthy of all the kind people who'd tried to pull him out of the mess and mire, he'd forgotten who had allowed him to be there in the first place. In fact, he wasn't even sure if he believed God existed anymore.

One thing was for certain. If He did exist, He didn't care about Jared De Luca. That was apparent. Everything he'd ever wanted and worked for had been taken away. His marriage with Jessica was only the latest example of that.

They'd had such plans for their marriage. They were going to go so far, him with his high-profile position in some exotic place like Miami, and Jessica with a PR firm representing big names. Jess had kept up her end of the plan. She'd made a name for herself in Hollywood. He couldn't blame her for dumping him when his career fizzled and he ended up in the backwater station of Riverside, California.

Still, the divorce papers had been a shock and had put his life in a nosedive. He'd faced the fact that they were never going to be the power couple they'd envisioned, but he always thought they would work it out... until she told him she'd found someone else. Someone she worked with in the PR firm. A man "much older and more established" she'd said. What she'd meant was the "perfect power partner."

Like a fool, he'd gone to Hollywood hoping to convince her to give it one more try before the court session. Their meeting was a pointless, painful debacle that ended in their divorce being finalized...and him not being there to answer Sam's call when he'd needed him. He'd failed. He should have been there to protect Sam.

End of sentence.

Sassa jerked and raised her head, her eyes blinking rapidly. Her hand shot to her neck.

"Owww." She rubbed the spot then scooted up in the seat and looked around. Cities and freeways had given way to the flat, open, golden hills of California's Central Valley.

"We're still an hour away from Kingsburg if you want to go back to sleep."

"No. My body hurts in every possible way. I'll sit up now." She pushed the button on the seat and the back popped forward. Scrubbing her face, she released a heavy sigh.

Jared felt that heartfelt sigh to the bottom of his toes. "I know." His voice was quiet. "I still can't believe he's gone, either."

She turned to face him. "You liked Sam a lot, didn't you?"

"He was a great man." No matter how sincere he sounded, Jared's tone couldn't match the feeling of loss inside him. It was like the day he'd lost his grandad, the only male parental figure he'd ever known.

What a shame he hadn't realized how much Sam had meant to him until now. A tight feeling clutched at his chest. "It may not seem like it, but I tried to protect him."

"You didn't try hard enough."

The hotheaded woman Sam had described—Sassy Sassa—was back. Her attitude even showed in her features. Those pouty lips thinned. Just a little, but enough to notice.

He wanted to say something, to come back with a smart remark, but he couldn't. What she'd said was true. He should have fought harder. Demanded more of…everything. Protection. Resources. Everything. Instead, he'd tried to go along with the program. Tried to be the dutiful agent, the good department man. He hadn't wanted to rock the boat or to make enemies of his superiors. Once again, trying to prove himself worthy. It was an ugly truth but one that needed to be faced.

Jared was about to admit that truth to Sassa when she shook her head. "I'm sorry. I shouldn't have said that. I'm guilty, too. I was close to Sam. I was his assistant. I should have known something was wrong. But I was wrapped up in my own issues."

A little surprised, he glanced her way and then quickly back to the freeway. "He worked hard to keep you out of it. He wanted to protect you and precious Keri."

She jerked in surprise. "That's what he called her."

Jared smiled for the first time in hours…or was it days? "I know. Sam talked about her a lot…and you."

He saw the glisten of tears before she turned her face away. "He was trying to save the world and I just wanted to save myself."

Her words gave Jared pause. "Did you need saving?"

Her little laugh was rueful. "Always. My life has been a series of setbacks. I had a full-ride scholarship for college, but no, I had to be one of the original teen moms. Pregnant in my senior year of high school. Then I married the guy." She shook her head.

"Kopack mentioned your ex has a gambling addiction."

She laughed again. "The appropriate question would be what isn't he addicted to? Women. Alcohol. I lost my first baby worrying over his addictions. Then Erik disappeared. When he came crawling back, I gave him a second chance."

She gave her ex a second chance? The one he never got. He turned to study her. "Why?"

Blue eyes widened and perky shaped brows rose into cute peaks.

"Why did you give him a second chance?" Jared repeated the question. The answer was important.

"I...guess I still loved him and... I believe marriage is a sacred vow."

Not the answer Jared had expected and a sound, almost a chuckle, slipped out.

Sassa turned to him. "Are you laughing at my beliefs?"

"No. I'm laughing at myself really. Do you know where I was when Sam called? I was in Los Angeles trying to convince my wife that we needed to give our marriage one more chance."

Sassa studied him for a long, silent moment. "Did it work?"

He gave his head a shake. "Just before we went into divorce court, her new boyfriend assured me there was nothing sacred about our vows...at least not for her."

"I'm sorry. That must have hurt."

She was quiet for a while. "I always felt that if Erik knew God, we would have had a better chance. But you can't force someone to see God...even if He's standing right in front of them."

"It would be better if He made Himself easier to see."

"It's not supposed to be easy. It's something we have to work toward."

"Is that why Sam's dead? To make life unbearably hard for you and me?"

Her lips parted then hardened as she faced forward, her eyes back on the road.

They drove for miles in silence.

Jared called himself several choice names. In her eyes, he'd just placed himself firmly in the camp of "those who can't see God." He couldn't afford to be there. He and this woman needed to be united. To stand together.

He shook his head. "We don't have time for this."

"For what?"

"Airing our different beliefs or indulging our…insecurities. Out of all the people in the world, Sam chose you and me to be his friends. He put his faith in us. We need to rally, to work together to save his legacy and maybe life as we know it. If the Black Knights release the virus, it will destroy crops around the world. Economies will collapse. People will starve. It will be a disaster."

"What can I do? You heard your boss, Kopack. I'm practically a suspect in Sam's murder."

Jared shook his head. "First, Kopack is not my boss. He's FBI, and he was just doing his job, which is to find the people who murdered Sam and stop them. Now we have to do our job."

She took a deep breath before asking, "And what exactly is our job?"

"I'm a border patrol officer. My job is to stop bioterrorism. You're a scientist. Your job is to find the problems and solve them."

"What do you mean?"

He glanced at her quickly. "Kopack is focused on finding the Black Knights and stopping them. He might not succeed. Then what happens?"

"They create the virus and release it."

"And it's our job to stop that from happening."

He saw her jerk before turning to stare at him. "You want me to find a cure for the virus."

He nodded. "Let Kopack find Chekhov and the Black Knights. You and I need to work on the cure. Sam started the job and I have access to his notes on our server."

"If you have the formula, you can put the best biologists on it. You don't need me."

He shook his head. "Yes, we do. After the breach to the computer system, Sam never trusted it. He refused to put the complete formula on our system."

"Then where did he put it?"

"We assumed he put all his final findings on a private computer, one he didn't hook up to the internet... ever."

"That's why Chekhov marched in and stole his computer bag. The formula is on that computer. But how did he know? If Sam was so careful, how did Chekhov know the formula was completed?"

"As far as I can tell, Chekhov *didn't* know Sam had completed the formula. I'm not sure he even knew Sam was working with us. I think Chekhov decided that Sam's trip to China was the perfect time to snatch June and then blackmail her husband into completing the virus. Once he kidnapped her and Sam alerted us, the

FBI and Homeland Security came into the investigation. Information shot across multiple networks. That's where we made our mistake. Until then, I don't think the Black Knights realized Sam had the formula. Once they did, they changed plans rapidly and devised a way to snatch it."

Sassa gave a little gasp. "June's dead, too, isn't she?"

"Kopack ordered a search warrant of their house as soon as he found out June was missing. Everything was in order. No broken furniture or anything else to indicate a struggle. We shouldn't assume she's dead."

Sassa eased back in her seat with a shudder. "The Black Knights have no reason to keep her alive if they have the formula and Sam is dead."

Miles and miles passed in silence. At last, Jared said, "You're the closest person to Sam's work. Now that it's in the hands of those maniacs, you're the only link we have to recreate it. You have to try."

He glanced over and met her wide, blue-eyed gaze. "Sam had faith in you. So do I."

Her lips parted in surprise. He kind of liked the look…a lot. The last thing he needed right now was to be distracted by pretty lips. He steeled his resolve and focused on the road ahead.

What he needed was to find a way to convince her he was right. To get her to agree—and that meant bridging the gap between them…the one he'd created.

They traveled the last few miles in silence before the Kingsburg water tower, quaintly formed in the shape of an antique Swedish coffee pot, came into view. It reminded him of Kingsburg's heritage…and Sassa's name.

"Your name…is it Swedish?"

She nodded but her voice was pitched low. "My family comes from a long line of Swedish settlers here in the valley."

"Sassa… It's very different. What does it mean?"

"It's a nickname really…for Astrid. But my mom likes it just the way it is."

"So do I. It suits you."

She made no response.

Well, that went well.

Ignoring the small frown that wreathed her features, he pulled off the freeway. They passed through the small town. The main street boasted a ton of Swedish motifs. Peaked roofs. Signs with Swedish names in curly, blue, geometric patterns. Bakeries offering delectable, unpronounceable delights. They drove past houses and stores into a predominantly agricultural area. Miles and miles of vineyards were broken only by orchards of pale peaches, plump apricots and bright oranges, leftovers from the summer season. Just enough fruit left from the harvest made the colors stand out against the dark bark and green leaves. A beautiful sight—and a stark reminder of what would be lost if the formula was developed.

They drove for miles out of town before Jared pulled into a large horseshoe driveway in front of a sprawling ranch-style house. Even before he shut down the engine, a couple exited the front door. Jared had called ahead to let the Nilssons know he was bringing their daughter home.

Sassa leaped out of the car. Jared followed as she ran to her mother, who carried an infant. The instant Sassa took the child into her arms, all the tightness and hard edges eased from her features. She smiled and

Jared almost stumbled. Her brilliant, beautiful smile transformed her. Golden sunshine slid out from behind a cloud and turned the somewhat dowdy, bedraggled creature into a glowing one. She exuded happiness and was more lovely than Jared had imagined she could ever be. He'd always heard motherhood did things to women, but he'd never witnessed it. Now that he had, he'd never forget it.

As he approached, the most beautiful small creature he had ever seen turned to look at him. Little blond curls nestled on top of her head. The biggest, bluest eyes peered at him with the kind of open curiosity only the very young can portray. He noted the pretty, pouty pink lips just like her mother's…then she smiled at him with the sweetest, most innocent look.

Precious Keri. That's what Sam had called her and now Jared understood why.

"Thank you for bringing her home to us." Sassa's father, Paul Nilsson, held out his hand.

Jared jumped to respond, trying desperately to shake off little Keri's charming ways. "You're welcome. It was the least I could do."

The FBI agents parked Sassa's car behind Jared's SUV and the other government vehicle pulled up behind it. One agent exited her vehicle and carried Sassa's luggage to where they all stood. Paul accepted the bag, stuffed the keys into his pocket, and thanked him. The man gave a terse nod then turned and headed back to the SUV. That was Jared's hint to move on.

"We need to go." He shook Paul's hand once again and turned to Sylvie Nilsson. She looked much like her daughter except that her blond hair was pulled into a tight bun at the back of her head. She'd kept one hand on her daughter from the moment Sassa was close enough to touch.

That's where Sassa gets her mothering instincts... from a woman who loves her unconditionally. A pang of something like envy swept through him.

Sylvie caught him staring and murmured her thanks.

Jared nodded and met Sassa's gaze. "The agents in that SUV will be keeping an eye on things around here. You'll be safe. I'll be in touch."

Understanding sparked between them. She nodded her head. "I'll be ready."

Relief swept through Jared and he dipped his head in recognition. Sassa was on board. Now they could get to work. He turned and walked back to his vehicle, but as he climbed in, he couldn't get the image of the three females—mother, daughter and baby—out of his mind. What would it be like to grow up in a loving family like this one? How would it feel to have such a rich heritage? He had no idea. But he knew one thing.

That kind of goodness needed preserving and he'd do everything in his power to make sure it happened.

TWO

"Mom, you absolutely have to go."

Her mother tugged on Keri's foot as the baby rested in Sassa's arms. "I feel like I'm abandoning you two in your greatest need."

Sassa felt the same way but she wouldn't openly admit it. After returning to her parents' home yesterday, she'd slept for a full twenty-four hours, waking just in time to pack and leave this morning. Her mother and father were flying to Florida for the birth of her brother's first child. They had driven into town in Sassa's car and were waiting for their Uber ride to pick them up.

This trip had been planned for ages and Sassa absolutely refused to be responsible for changing it now. She was one-hundred-percent certain her brother had taken the job across the country to get away from her ongoing issues. Not that he didn't love Sassa. He did. But he had a life of his own and her constant "crisis mode" life consumed everyone.

Lars and his wife, Sherry, deserved her parents' undivided attention for this big event. And besides, the farther they were away, the safer they'd be. If she could find an excuse, she'd send Keri with them. But if she did that, her mother would suspect things weren't as safe as Sassa had claimed.

Still, they needed to go now, before she broke down and sobbed out the truth.

She sent her dad a pleading glance. Even though her mother seemed oblivious, Dad understood her need. Putting his arm around his wife, he gently pulled her away. "We will miss our plane if we don't get moving. The Uber we ordered is here."

Shifting Keri, Sassa wrapped an arm around her dad's waist. "Thanks."

He kissed the top of her head and murmured, "I've got your back, Sass, always."

Her mother threw her arms around both her and Keri for one huge hug. "Watch that tooth in the front. I think it's ready to break through. She's been chewing on her fist like crazy. Be careful…and listen to Agent De Luca. I think he really cares. I'll be praying for you."

Sassa tried to get Keri to wave to Grandma as she hurried to the waiting car. The baby turned big blue eyes toward her as if to ask "what's going on?" but she refused to wave.

"Mommy and Grandma are trying not to cry. Someday you'll understand." She waved one last time then nodded at the FBI agents parked in a car across the street.

Agent Kopack's assigned men were still watching over her. Were they there for her protection or to make sure she didn't run? She wasn't sure but she was thankful for their presence.

She hurried into her small Craftsman bungalow and wrinkled her nose at the musty, closed-up smell. Despite the slight odor, Sassa released a grateful sigh. Being home felt good.

Her parents had helped her purchase the tiny, renovated Craftsman cottage close to the university. Built in the twenties, the house had been restored by the previous owners and now rested in a small enclave of older houses, all restored and in pristine condition.

She loved her little home with its front porch, big windows, wood floors and stained glass in the transom above the front door. This was her safe haven, her hope…a sign that she might finally be getting her head above the waves of insecurity that had almost swamped her.

But today she couldn't slow down long enough to enjoy being home. She hadn't told her parents, but she was headed to the university. The sooner she got to work, the better.

Grabbing diapers from Keri's room and fresh bottles, she stuffed them into her diaper bag just as her cell phone rang. Jared's name flashed on the screen. Apparently he'd programmed his number into it before he'd returned it to her.

"Hello?"

"Are you home?" Jared's deep voice rumbled through the phone. Any other time she might have found it attractive…or not. She liked the sound of his voice, so she probably would have argued and used his abrupt manner to make a smart reply. But too much had happened. She took his urgency to heart.

"Yes. What's wrong?"

"I'll be there in five minutes."

She hung up. Something was wrong—seriously wrong. Picking up Keri, she headed out the front door to wait for him on the porch.

He pulled the black government SUV alongside the

curb in front of her house and exited. As he made his way toward her, she noted his broad shoulders again.

What was wrong with her? She went out of her way not to notice men, especially too handsome ones like her ex-husband, Erik. She suspected the officer was one of those charming guys who knew how to win a girl over. Besides, he was an unbeliever like her ex, and she wanted to be as far away from that kind of doubt as possible. These days, she coveted the comfort and companionship of people of faith.

Jared's clouded features told her she'd been right. Something was wrong. A deep frown creased his forehead and his dark eyes seemed darker at a distance.

"What is it? What's happened?" Neither of them had time for niceties.

He stopped in front of her and grasped her elbow almost as if to support her.

"They've found June Kruger, Sassa. She's dead."

She sagged and was thankful for his hand on her arm. Taking two steps back, she fell into her cushioned rattan chair.

"I knew it. I just knew it. Where did they find her?"

Jared bowed his head. "Floating in a canal."

"Oh, no…no. How horrible!" She sobbed. Tears fell down her cheeks. Keri puckered and tears formed in her eyes.

Sassa sniffed and gave the little one a gentle hug. "It's all right, baby. Mommy's all right."

But she wasn't. She was miserable and frightened and of no use to her daughter.

Jared crouched in front of them. "It's all right, precious Keri." His use of Sam's endearment made Sassa's tears fall harder.

"It's not all right! Everything is awful! What kind of animals would do that to June?"

Keri began to cry in earnest. Sassa made a sound and clutched her daughter to her chest. "I'm sorry, baby. So sorry."

"Come on. Let's go inside." He helped Sassa from the chair, his arm the only thing keeping her up because her legs refused to work properly again. He led her to the sofa and eased her down, then hurried to the kitchen. Cabinet doors opened and the faucet turned on. He came back with a glass of water and a box of tissues. The house belonged to her, but she wasn't even sure where he'd found the items. He knelt in front of her again.

Her thoughts were jumbled. *Please, Lord.* She didn't even know what she was pleading for.

Her nose was running. Everything was a blur…except her crying baby. She wiped her cheeks. "I'm all right, sweetheart. See?" She smiled—a watery lift of her lips—and Keri's whimpers eased but her poor little mouth stayed down-turned. Sassa snatched a tissue from the box and wiped Keri's cheeks and then her own. Finally she took the glass of cold water from Jared and sipped. Keri reached for Sassa's face, her gaze still doubtful.

"Come on, Keri, give us a smile." Jared reached over and tickled a place under the child's little chin. She shrugged her shoulder and the frown turned up—not much, but it was a glimmer of a smile. She studied Jared with an oh-so-serious gaze.

"That's better. A few more minutes of those puckered lips and I'd be crying, too."

Sassa laughed. She couldn't help it. The image of tall, wide-shouldered Officer De Luca in tears was too much.

Keri reached for the shiny badge on his shirt and he leaned in closer. A light aftershave, faint but still there, sifted through Sassa's stuffy nose. Pine, fresh and clean. Suddenly, Sassa was all too aware of handsome, manly Officer De Luca's closeness.

Reaching for his badge, Keri tipped forward and fell into his arms. Sassa couldn't help smiling at the look on Jared's face. He caught the baby and held her up for a single, startled moment before gingerly placing her on one broad thigh. Fascinated by the bright badge on his chest, Keri ignored the big man behind it, so Sassa took the opportunity to blow her nose and pull in a deep breath. But her momentary break didn't last long. Keri looked up at Jared, pulled wet fingers out of her mouth and reached for his dark beard. Jared caught the slimy little hand midway and awkwardly pushed the baby back into Sassa's lap.

Jerking to his feet, he wiped wet fingers on his pants. "Agent Kopack wants us over at the Kruger residence. We need to get going."

Sassa looked like she had yesterday in San Francisco. Numb. Moving automatically. Her stunned features made Jared feel guilty, so when she lifted the baby's bag off the couch, he took it from her and moved outside. He transferred Keri's car seat to his SUV. Sassa's car would probably stay parked until this was over. More than likely, Sassa would not be using it until then.

The Kruger residence wasn't far away and would have been hard to miss even if Jared hadn't been given the address. Black government vehicles blocked the quiet, upscale street. A group of neighbors stood outside a yellow-taped perimeter.

Sassa hopped out, pulled Keri from her car seat and slung the backpack over her shoulders. He was amazed at how quickly she had gathered herself. Still, her body seemed rigid and stiff, as if she was tensed for whatever lay ahead.

The guard at the front door stopped them until he received a signal from someone inside. When he stepped back, allowing them access, they moved into the house.

The place had been demolished. Pillows and cushions slashed open. Large lamps smashed on the ground. Every shelf, every piece of furniture, had been turned over, torn apart or destroyed.

Sassa gasped. "Oh, no."

Jared glanced at her. She clasped Keri close and those pretty, pouty, pink lips trembled. Her armor had slipped. She looked vulnerable and close to the edge. She'd already been through so much. She didn't need this. He wanted to reach out to her but knew she wouldn't appreciate it. Instead, he gritted his teeth and searched the room for Kopack.

The man walked toward them, a stack of papers in his hand. Jared didn't waste time.

"You could have given us some warning."

Kopack sighed. "We're just as surprised as you, De Luca. We were here two days ago, right after Dr. Kruger notified us that his wife was missing. It didn't look like this."

"They did this after…?"

He nodded. "Maybe last night. A neighbor thought she saw something, a flash of lights. She contacted the local police. When they arrived, things were silent. No sign of lights or intruders. We didn't find this wreckage until this morning after the police discovered June's body. We came back here looking for clues and found this." He gestured to the demolished room. "It appears they were trying to open a safe. The police scared them off before they could finish. Our people just got it cracked open. These documents were inside. We'd like you to take a look, Ms. Nilsson. Maybe it's the professor's formula for the pathogen."

Sassa took the papers and looked around for a place to sit. Obviously, she couldn't hold her daughter and shift the papers. Finding no available spot, she handed Keri to Jared.

Surprised, he shifted the baby in his arms. First thing she did was reach for his badge.

Good thing to know. Babies like bright, shiny objects.

He moved her again. She weighed less than his workout bag, but she was wiggly and made him nervous. He placed his hand on her back to keep her from toppling. The action pulled her closer and a sweet, powdery scent drifted upward. Nice. Clean.

Sassa shuffled the papers. "It is some kind of formula for sure. Give me a moment." She read silently. Jared picked his way through the debris to the safe behind the picture. Not a very discreet hiding place. Sam had been so cautious about everything else. Why would he put the formula in such a low-grade safety receptacle with an obvious location?

He studied the front of the small safe. The lock buttons were in a straight row instead of a square. Unusual. Sam must've paid a pretty penny for that unique setup.

Ten square blocks, zero to nine. Something about them tickled his memory. The ID bracelet! The one Sam had been so determined to give to Sassa. Did it mean something?

At that moment Keri lost interest in his badge and reached up, determined to stick her fingers in his mouth. He grasped her little hand, held it down and turned to the men in the room. "Sassa, do you have the bracelet? I think the numbers on it might be the combination."

All the men in the room paused and stared. Kopack shook his head. "What does it matter? The safe is open."

"Sam insisted Sassa take the bracelet with his last breath. She already knew he wanted her to have it. So why was it so important?" He shook his head. "Sam was purposeful. That bracelet meant more to him than just a keepsake. I want to know what."

Kopack nodded. "Good idea, De Luca. Looks like you might carry your weight around here, after all."

The comment struck deep but Jared refused to react. Everywhere he went he had to prove himself. Did he wear a sign on his forehead that read Lost Cause Who Doesn't Even Know His Own Father? His past seemed to be something other men could smell—and it followed him everywhere he went. All he'd ever wanted was to prove his grandfather's faith in him, to be worthy of the kindness the officer of his youth had showed him. If he could do that, maybe he'd finally earn his wife's respect. Maybe…

He pushed the thought away. He'd refused to respond to Kopack's remark, but he didn't miss the slight frown that creased Sassa's brow. Apparently, she didn't like Kopack's dig, either.

Was Sassy Sassa about to defend Jared? The thought made him smile. That big chip on her shoulder might come in handy sometimes.

The smile faded when Kopack turned to Sassa. "Do you know the number, Miss Nilsson?"

"No, but I have the bracelet." Reaching into the pocket of her jeans, she pulled out the large, man's bracelet. Her hand looked delicate and fragile against the heavy, bulky links. She handed the object to Kopack. He carried it to the technician who had opened the safe. The drilled-out lock sat inside the open door. The man reconnected the wires from the loose lock to the back of the safe door then punched in the numbers.

No sound. No click. Nothing.

He punched the numbers one more time then shook his head. "It's not the code for this safe."

"You're sure it's not just damaged?" Kopack asked.

"Definitely. Something would have registered if it was the right code."

Hope faded in Jared. Well, it *was* a good idea.

Sassa lifted the papers. "I'm afraid this destruction was all for nothing. These files are research for Xylella, but it's our initial work. We were trying to find a cure for X when we created the new pathogen. I don't know why Sam felt the need to lock these papers up. They're public knowledge. They've already been published."

Kopack nodded. "It seems he put all of his important papers in the safe. We found these, too." He handed her a manila envelope.

"What's this?"

"It's Dr. Kruger's will. On the envelope is the name and number of his attorney and…the executor of his estate. You."

Sassa frowned and her voice dropped a notch. "Sam had everything in order. Do you think he expected to die?"

Kopack agreed. "It seems he was prepared for all possibilities…except how far the Knights were willing to go to obtain the information. None of us imagined they'd make such a public move and murder him in front of witnesses."

Jared clamped down on the words *I believed it and I warned you.* Instead he said, "The important thing to remember is they have gone public. They'll never be able to go back underground. This is their last gambit, a suicidal bid for their group. We can't underestimate them again. They won't stop until they've introduced that pathogen into the world."

And Sassa Nilsson is our only hope for stopping it.

He didn't say the words out loud, but it was apparent that same thought was on the mind of everyone in the room…except Sassa. She seemed focused elsewhere. He could almost see the wheels churning behind her unfocused gaze.

Keri chose that moment to reach for his mouth again. Jared grabbed her tiny hand and looked down into big, beautiful, blue eyes, just like her mother's. The beginnings of a smile tickled the corners of her baby-doll lips, also like Sassa's. He couldn't imagine Nikolai Chekhov getting his hands on the helpless little bundle in his arms…or her mother. Sassa might have some prickly edges but she didn't deserve what that madman would dish out.

Jared halted the scenarios his imagination created before they could take shape. But a new and fierce determination to stop Chekhov and his organization took root within him.

"Wait a minute!" Sassa glanced around, a hopeful glint in her gaze. "If Sam had sent these documents to his lawyer, is it possible he sent him the formula, too?"

"We thought of that and we've contacted his lawyer.

He's en route to his office now. In the meantime, we need to double your guard."

"My guard? Why?"

Jared took a deep breath. "It's been a crazy week for you, Sassa. You haven't really had time to put two and two together."

"Two and two about what?"

He glanced at Kopack then back to the intense question in Sassa's blue eyes. "You heard what he said. The Kruger residence was in perfect condition when they searched it at the beginning of the week. Last night someone trashed it. Think about it, Sassa. The Black Knights already had Sam's computer. So what were they looking for when they trashed the house?"

Her blue eyes widened. "The formula wasn't on his computer."

"Exactly."

She gave a brief shake of her head. "I knew that. If I'd thought about it, I knew it. I put his conference notes on that computer myself. It was a simple little thing. If there'd been a locked file or something unusual on it, I would have seen."

"Obviously, Sam hid the formula someplace else."

"But where? It's not in the lab. I know every inch of that place. I'd know if it was hidden there. It wasn't in Sam's safe or anyplace here in the house. Where could it be?"

"We don't know and neither do the Black Knights."

She frowned, and Jared sighed. Her brain was on overload because her normally sharp mind was taking a long time to pull the pieces together.

He hated to do it, but he had to speed up the process. She needed to be aware.

"That means, Sassa, you are the only living link to the formula's location. You're also the only one who has a chance of repeating the formula or creating a cure. I'm afraid you just became number one on the Black Knights' Most Wanted list. Kopack needs to double your protection and I won't be leaving your side."

Jared suggested she might want to go home, but Sassa insisted on going straight to the lab. Her decision seemed to please him and he smiled. A good smile. White teeth against his dark beard. Strong and sincere. He'd given her a slightly sarcastic grin on the car trip home, but this was different. This smile was real—the first she'd seen on him—and a little thrill speared through her whole being. She'd brought one bright spot into his day. That was a good thing. They'd no doubt have too few of those in the time ahead.

They were dropping Keri off at the campus childcare center when one of the FBI agents assigned to watch Sassa planted himself in a corner of the playroom. Sassa sent a worried glance in Jared's direction.

"It's just a precaution I suggested and since I'll be by your side, we can afford to leave one of your guards here. Kopack agreed."

Still...

Sassa sent one last, worried glance toward her daughter before Jared ushered her out the door for the walk across campus.

When she finally stepped through the door of the lab, Sam's three assistants, Matt, Libby and Jacki, stopped what they were doing and turned to her.

Okay. Another hurdle. She was in charge now. They waited.

She took a breath.

"Thank you all for being here. I think you're aware of what's happening."

Matt, the oldest of the lab assistants, nodded. "The FBI has been here setting up equipment since yesterday." He nodded at Sam's glass-enclosed office. "The IT guy is in there now."

Stalling for time, Sassa nodded, slipped her lab coat off the hanger near the door and put it on. Then she ran her favorite citrus-flavored lip balm over her lips. Only then did she meet the steady gaze of her fellow workers. She hesitated, trying to decide what to tell them. Fortunately, she had Sam's lead to follow. That meant nothing but the truth. "I think we all know Dean Trujillo is not a fan of Sam's program. Now that he's gone, our jobs here are most likely in jeopardy. I want to give you warning… in case we're not successful in recreating the pathogen."

"We will be." Matt spoke before she could go on. "You'll find a way. We know you will."

Their confidence warmed Sassa. She didn't know what to say, how to express her appreciation. She looked up. Jared, arms folded over his chest, leaned against the doorjamb of Sam's office. A satisfied smile floated over his lips. That little half smile vote of confidence did funny things to her stomach—made it flip—and brought a flush to her cheeks.

Exactly the kind of response she didn't need to have to Mr. Jared De Luca but…the fate of the world was sitting on her shoulders. She needed all the help she could get.

She allowed herself that little moment of pleasure. Told herself it would be just one. Later, she'd put Jared's smile and his confidence in the box where they belonged—with all the other good-looking, charming unbelievers in the world. But right now, his faith in her gave her strength.

She nodded at her fellow workers. "Let's get to work then…for Sam."

"For Sam," they repeated.

"I'll need all of your notes and lab assignments from the days before the accident. Anything that might jog our memories or point us in the right direction. I want to make sure we all observed the same things and, also, to make sure I didn't miss some small detail."

They returned to their desks and Sassa headed to Sam's office. Jared was blocking the door and didn't move. She looked up. A wry smile played around his lips, surprisingly full ones for a man. She shouldn't notice things like that. Couldn't afford to notice them. Sassa ducked her head as if to push her way through, but he didn't move. And she didn't dare step any closer. He smelled too good. Like fresh pines. Because he refused to move, she was forced to look up.

"You can do this, Sassa. Even your colleagues believe in you."

She ducked her head again. This time a smile wavered across her own lips. "Actually, I am a pretty good biologist. I guess it's just my family I keep letting down."

He frowned. "From what I've seen, your family is very proud of you. You haven't let them down."

She made a small sound. "I thought I had a bright future. That's all down the drain now. If the FBI wasn't backing me, I'm sure Dean Trujillo would have kicked me off the campus. He never liked me."

"I take it Sassy Sassa made an appearance during one of your encounters with the man?"

Laughter escaped before she could stop it. "I think you spent entirely too much time talking to Sam."

He folded his arms tighter. "I wish I'd spent more time. Now it's too late."

"Yes…for both of us." She took a deep breath and looked around. "All I ever wanted was to support my daughter, to take care of her without the world constantly falling down around me."

He straightened from leaning on the jamb and lifted her chin with his finger. "You didn't create this disaster."

"No. I didn't. But it's up to me to fix it." Her words sounded a little shaky…like she felt.

Jared took a deep breath. "My grandfather had a favorite scripture he always used to quote when I felt like I was in over my head. Jeremiah 29, verse eleven. He made me memorize it so I could repeat it. 'For I know the thoughts that I think toward you…thoughts of peace, and not of evil, to give you an expected end.'"

She looked up. His brown eyes were deep, dark and sincere. "I thought you said you don't believe."

His lips twisted in a wry smile. "I'm not sure I do. But you do and you're ruining my good story, so listen up. My granddad would always finish the scripture by saying, 'You don't know what His plans are for you, but you can be sure He never sends the wrong man for the job.'"

"You think I'm the right person for the job?"

Jared nodded. "You are. And don't forget, it's not all up to you. It's us. I won't leave you alone in this."

Us. The last time somebody said "us" to her, it turned out to be a disaster. She would never forget that again. No matter how appealing Jared made it sound, there would never be an "us" for her.

She stepped forward, trying to push her way through, but he wouldn't budge.

"It's been a rough morning. I think you need a pick-me-up. How about a cup of coffee?"

"I'm more of a tea drinker."

"Okay, can I get you something else?"

Her laugh was rueful. "What I would really love to have is something I absolutely don't need."

"What's that?"

"I could eat a dozen *hallongrotta* from my favorite Kingsburg bakery. You know…raspberry caves? Yummy shortbread cookies with raspberry jam in the center?"

"Yeah, I've seen those." He paused and a doubtful frown creased the place between his brows. "A dozen all by yourself?"

Now. Right now was the perfect time to set their relationship back on the right course. Time to cut through all the nice words and the hopeful pulse-pounding smiles. She met his gaze squarely. "You don't think I got these hips from eating like a mouse, do you? I'm a stress eater. So, yes, a dozen cookies all by myself."

Surprise flitted over his features, but he didn't rush in to contradict her or to feed her false compliments. Sassa knew the truth about herself. She was short and rounder than most women. Years of stress eating had added on the pounds and she'd never been able to shed the extra baby fat. Probably never would. She had no illusions about herself and she hoped Jared didn't foster any, either. She would be sorely disappointed in him if he did.

She had no illusions about him finding her attractive in any way. His wife was probably tall, slender, dark-haired with lovely dusky skin. And immaculately put together.

Just the opposite of Sassa's thrown-together, baby-on-her-hip usual style. She knew the truth and hoped Jared wouldn't try to make her feel good with a bunch of insincere compliments she could see right through.

He didn't. He kept silent.

What a relief. And yet…a tinge of disappointment crowded the edges of her awareness.

He could have protested just a little.

And that's exactly why you have to keep your distance, girl. You always fall for his kind. Now put that nonsense behind you and get on with the real issue.

"I'm ready for you now, Ms. Nilssen," the computer technician called out.

Relieved, Sassa pushed around Jared's silent form. As she sat at the desk, she glanced up once to see his frowning features before the tech explained the FBI's equipment and the log-on procedure.

After a few moments, Jared turned and left. He flung the outer lab door open and gave a little salute to the guards outside. Sassa forced herself not to watch the portal close behind him.

Jared glanced at the two boxes on the car seat beside him—little white boxes with curling blue designs tied with a blue ribbon. Each box held a dozen *hallongrotta*, one whole box for Sassa and one for the other lab technicians.

After the half hour drive to Kingsburg, he'd easily figured out which bakery on the small town's main street he needed to visit. He just looked for the most customers and parked cars. Apparently, the bakery was a local favorite. Half an hour to return to the lab and almost as much time to find a parking spot. The university semester was in full swing during March. He had to park nearly a mile away. He hurried to the lab, shaking his head. An hour and a half to buy cookies.

But it would be worth it to see Sassa's face.

He'd been uncomfortable with her attitude and the comment about her hips. Nothing was wrong with Sassa Nilsson. She had gorgeous eyes, pretty lips, long blond hair some women would kill for and yes...she was curvy. That's the word he would use. *Curvy.* It suited her. So, if she needed a full box of raspberry-filled cookies to get through the day, then she would get her cookies.

Besides, the sweets might ease the news he'd been holding back. He hadn't wanted to give her the info he'd received earlier from Kopack. She'd already had a rough morning. He hoped the box of cookies would soften the news.

He entered the lab. Sassa came out of Sam's office. She'd twisted her long hair up into a knot and stuck a pencil through it to keep it in place. Small tendrils had escaped the back and the sides, little wisps that brushed against her cheeks. Her white lab coat flopped down around the knees of her jeans and she had a distracted air about her, like her mind wasn't on where she was going as she studied the papers in her hand.

She glanced up. "Good. You're here. I need to run home to pick up some things and get Keri's travel bed. We'll be staying here tonight.

"Here? At the lab?"

Still distracted, she glanced up again. "Yes. We've done it before. Keri's young enough she doesn't get into things and I can keep her close."

He studied her. "You've discovered something."

A slight frown crossed her brow as she read the papers. "I think so, but I want to crunch the numbers. I hadn't realized Sam had instructed Matt to double the amount of X on one of the slides. If they all broke…that means it mixed triple the amount of the virus. I don't know. It could be significant. Anyway, it'll be easier if I stay in the lab tonight, but I have to pick up Keri. The child-care center won't hold her after five. Most classes are over by that time. I'll grab what I need from home, get some dinner and head right back here."

"I'll come with you."

"That's not necessary."

"Yes, it is."

She finally looked up from the papers. Her gaze landed on the boxes in his hands. "What are those?"

"Raspberry caves."

Her lips parted and her hands lowered. "You went all the way to Kingsburg?"

He shrugged. "I told you. We're in this together. If my partner needs a box of *hallongrotta*, my partner gets a box of *hallongrotta*."

A slow, sweet smile, one he had only seen her share with Keri, slipped onto her face. Did that little lift mean she understood his subliminal message…that she was fine just the way she was? Or would she think it was a ploy to keep her on task? That was partly true. But he meant every word about them being partners. He would not fail her like he'd failed Sam.

"Thank you…that was kind, but I don't really need them."

"You might."

Her smile faded. "What do you mean?"

"Kopack called. Sam's pastor is trying to reach the

executor of Sam's estate to make…funeral arrangements."

Jared stumbled over the word *funeral*. It was hard for him to say and it crushed Sassa. Her eyes closed and her stance wavered for one long moment. Then, with trembling fingers, she unbuttoned the lab coat and tossed it in a bin near the door. Grabbing her jacket, she slammed open the door and strode down the hall.

Jared was hard-pressed to keep up with her, but he knew where she was going. He lengthened his stride and walked beside her. The FBI agents assigned to watch over Sassa fell into step behind them as they crossed the campus to the child-care center. Inside the small facility, they waited at the counter for the assistant to fetch Keri. Sassa stared at the room with a dazed, on-the-brink look. She seemed about to tumble over the edge. How could he anchor her and keep her grounded?

The assistant crossed the room and handed Sassa her baby. She clasped her daughter to her like she was a life vest in an angry sea. The baby—instinctive, wise little creature that she was—reached both hands up to clasp her mother's face. Sassa closed her eyes and touched her forehead to her daughter's. Mother and baby held each other close.

Jared's heart jolted. He'd just witnessed one of the most beautiful sights he'd ever seen.

THREE

Tule fog covered the cemetery. In winter it formed from the Tule grasslands and blanketed the Central Valley. Sometimes the mist was so thick, it could be seen from outer space. The fog was also the leading cause of weather-related accidents in the valley. Jared didn't know where he'd read those details. He only knew that it seemed appropriate that the sky should go gray on the day they lay June and Sam Kruger in the ground.

A great man and woman were lost to the world. Jared desperately fought his tears throughout the funeral. Beside him, Sassa cried unabashedly. Jessica would have hidden behind a black hat or a scarf. She never would have let the world see her pain. But Sassa stood boldly, her eyes puffy, her nose red, her long hair curling and frizzing in the mist and wept her heart out for the people she loved.

To be so open, so honest about her emotions, and so passionate about people, made her beautiful in Jared's eyes. And he'd never admired her more than he did, standing beside her as she said goodbye to her friends and jostled her confused and antsy child.

Keri knew something was wrong. Every once in a

while, she'd tilt her head and look into her mother's face, trying to understand and figure out the puzzle. The invisible bond he'd witnessed before was just as strong, just as mystifying and just as beautiful. But after more than an hour, Sassa was worn thin and Keri was trying to crawl out of her arms.

He knew Sassa wouldn't appreciate it but she looked about to drop. He reached for Keri. To his surprise, the baby jumped into his arms. He'd worn a suit today, so no shiny badge to entertain her, but she seemed content to fall back on her favorite pastime—trying to stick her fingers in his mouth. Even more surprising, when he put his arm around Sassa's shoulder and pulled her close, she leaned into him as if she was thankful for his support.

He held them both, wishing he could ease their pain…ease his own pain.

Sam and June were gone. Nothing would change that. Nothing. The emptiness of eternity filled his being with sorrow.

The caskets rested over graves dug on each side of their son. Christopher Kruger's tall, gray-marble headstone stood as a lone sentinel in the middle. Someone had sent a square, flat arrangement of flowers to sit in front of his marker. The white lilies and roses were a direct contrast to the simple gray stone, adorned only with Christopher's name, date of birth and death. Below his name, there was a line of ten small, colored-glass squares.

Why ten in a straight line, like Sam's safe? The squares were tasteful and added a splash of life to the gray stone, but the similarity to the safe in Sam's house jumped out at Jared.

Why, Sam? What were you trying to say?

The squares were a simple decoration on an otherwise blank stone. Nothing else. No hidden clue. No warning. Was he looking for answers where there were no questions? Hoping his brilliant, remarkable friend had left him a crumb to follow?

No bolt of lightning flashed from the sky to illuminate him. No small voice whispered in his mind.

Sam was gone…and it seemed to Jared that God was, too.

He'd listened carefully to the pastor's words, hoping something would give him comfort. Wishing some glimmer of light would flash into the bleak, gray sky. He wanted some warmth, some sign. But nothing came and he remembered Sassa's words.

It's not supposed to be easy.

But why must it be so hard?

He looked up. No answers came from the heavens. No small voice responded. Nothing brought him comfort.

The crowd in dark clothes, huddled beneath umbrellas, spread out over the area. So many people. So much loss. He barely heard the last of the pastor's sermon but dutifully bowed his head in the final prayer. He tensed as the service ended and mourners made their way toward Sassa, the closest person to Sam and June. First came the other lab assistants, then friends of June's came to see Keri, the child June had treated like her own grandchild.

A sharp pain pierced Jared's chest. He took a deep breath and looked away, simply to keep the tears at bay. A man crossed an empty clearing in front of him, headed to the line of greeters waiting to speak to Sassa.

He wore dark clothes and glasses in the sunless sky and something about him looked familiar.

A mourner said something to Jared and reached to shake his hand. Jared looked down and nodded in response as his mind tried to place where he'd seen the man before.

Sunglasses in a sunless sky. Just like Chekhov the day he murdered Sam.

Suddenly a photo flashed in his memory and he looked up. The man had moved behind the line, out of Jared's view, but he caught a glimpse of a long ponytail.

Jacob Heiser, the former Mossad agent suspected of two political assassinations, who now served as Chekhov's right-hand man. He was here…now.

Jared clasped Keri tighter and jerked Sassa away from the person she was reaching to hug. Pulling her back, he searched for Kopack, who stood slightly behind them.

"Jacob Heiser is here. At the back of the line."

Kopack stiffened, his gaze shooting over the crowd. Jared glanced back over his shoulder. Heiser must have realized he'd been seen. He broke free from the crowd, shoving people out of the way as he ran in the opposite direction and disappeared over a grass rise into the fog.

Kopack's shouts rang over the crowd. "Get her to the car!"

Agents jumped into action. Two ran forward, grabbed Sassa's arms and hurried her toward their SUV. One tried to take Keri from Jared, but he jerked her close and ran for the SUV. The agent followed as Kopack's group dashed past them, pushing through the crowd that had begun to scatter. The mourners were well aware that Sam and June had been murdered. The agents' drastic action and fierce response created chaos and fear. Everyone was desperate to get away.

People jostled and shoved. A woman cried out and fell to the ground. A man shouted and tried to lift her.

Sassa was ahead of Jared. She looked back, over her shoulder at the scene. Her face was a mask of horror as more people scrambled and fled the funeral site. The look on her face bit deep into Jared.

The agents opened the back door of the SUV. Sassa slid in, with Jared right behind her. She took Keri out of his arms and stared back the way they'd come. The agents piled into the front and locked the doors.

They were safe inside but Sassa still clutched the baby to her chest. Her breathing sounded loud and heavy in the silence.

"It's all right. These vehicles are reinforced. They can't get to us here."

She nodded but never spoke, her gaze glued to where the coffins rested, partially hidden by the fog that drifted back and forth. Slowly, the shouts faded away. The fog thinned and the graves reappeared. A dark blue ribbon on a wreath of flowers flapped in the breeze. The pastor, obviously nervous, edged his way back to bless each newly turned grave with trembling hands. The funeral director, looking flustered and confused, joined him as well as a representative from the cemetery. The minister finished his private blessing just as Kopack and his men came back over the hill, without Heiser.

Jared gritted his teeth. He looked at Sassa. "Stay here."

She nodded. He slipped out and waited for the distinct click of car doors locking before he made his way to Kopack. The agent held a phone to his ear so Jared addressed Agent Paulsen.

"Heiser got away?"

Paulsen nodded, still trying to catch his breath. "He had a car waiting for him. The driver sped away before we could get there. We didn't dare take a shot with all these people running around in the fog."

"Did you get a license plate number?"

The agent nodded at Kopack. "He's sending it in now. But I wouldn't get my hopes up. I'm sure the car was stolen."

Probably true, but it made Heiser's actions even more confusing. "Why now? Why would he risk coming here in the middle of the service?"

"I don't know." The man shrugged. "Serial killers often attend a funeral to see the results of their crime. Maybe that's what this guy had on his mind."

Jared shook his head. "That's not Heiser's or Chekhov's modus operandi. If Heiser was here, he had a reason. But what?"

The Black Knights were most certainly watching Sassa. They'd know she never left the lab and would assume she was working on the formula. Were they hoping to snatch her in the midst of the emotional situation at the funeral?

No. Heiser wasn't trying to get close to Sassa. He was trying to blend into the crowd, trying not to be seen. If the fog hadn't cleared at the perfect moment, Jared wouldn't have spotted him. But still, it was a risk. Why?

His gaze landed on Christopher Kruger's headstone. The similarity to the safe in Sam's house struck him again. He strode toward the very emotional funeral director. When the man saw Jared coming, he stepped back, almost in fear.

Jared raised a hand in an attempt to reassure the stressed and anxious man. "What can you tell me about Christopher Kruger's headstone?"

Surprised, the director hesitated. "Well, I know Mr. Kruger special ordered it and preordered two more exactly like it, one for himself and another for his wife."

"He ordered all three at the same time. Is that typical?"

"For most people, no. But it is fairly typical for parents of children who die before them. They want to be together in eternity."

Jared nodded. Being together in eternity was another of those things he wasn't sure he believed anymore. Ignoring the little spikes of doubtful resentment that popped up, he asked, "Was there anything unusual about the order?"

"I don't believe so, but we didn't place the order ourselves. Mr. Kruger asked for references and I gave him a list of manufacturers. He had it delivered to us when it was completed. We sent it over here for installation." He looked at the cemetery worker.

Jared turned to the other man. "Nothing strange or unusual with the installation?"

"Not at all. Mr. Kruger visited daily. I'm sure if there was a problem, he would have alerted us."

That caught Jared's attention. "He was here daily?"

"Yes, he visited every morning before he went to work."

"Did you notice anything unusual in his behavior in the last few weeks?"

"My workers didn't report anything... However..."

He hesitated again. "I don't think it has anything to do with the Kruger gravesite in particular but we've begun to have a high volume of vandalism at various gravesites. We were forced to increase night security."

"Were the Kruger plots vandalized?"

The cemetery worker shook his head. "No, not that I'm aware. We think it was a group of kids, choosing to hang out here. They discarded liquor bottles and tore up flower arrangements and mementos. Nothing serious. Just mischief. The activities have halted since we added the extra security."

Another dead end. Jared's hope sank. "Thank you— and thank you for your efforts here today."

Both men nodded. The funeral director's sigh conveyed both frustration and appreciation.

Jared headed for the SUV, no closer to an answer than when he'd left.

Sassa cleansed the glass slides one last time and slid them back into the container. Disappointment swept through her as her latest great idea came to nothing. She ran her lip balm over dry lips. So far, she had not been able to repeat Sam's experiment and re-create the virus. She was running out of ideas and feeling less like the brilliant associate Jared described and more like her old self, the one who couldn't do things right.

The Black Knights' constant harassment hadn't helped her stress level. The building where the lab was located was an older one, two stories, with classrooms on the lower level and the lab and offices on the upper. The FBI agents were stationed right outside Sassa's door. One day, an altercation between two male students near the stairs forced them to move out of position. Jared had heard the commotion and stepped into their place to see two men he didn't recognize walking toward him from the opposite end of the corridor.

When he drew his gun, they stepped into a nearby office and disappeared…from a two-story building with one opening…the door they had entered.

Once the altercation with the students was settled, the agents had searched the office and found an open window with a lightweight cord trailing to the ground. No doubt the men were Black Knights members with a mission who were prepared for all contingencies. In addition, the FBI had questioned the students who had created the disturbance only to discover they'd been paid one hundred dollars each by a stranger to create a distraction.

On another day there was a power outage in the building. The main fuse panel had been tampered with—not enough to require major repairs, just enough to irritate Sassa and slow her work.

After the power kicked back on, it was a long time before Sassa's computer whirred back to life. She feared she'd lost all her work.

These were smaller incidents, just enough to keep Kopack and his agents hopping. But Sassa was certain the incidents were orchestrated by the Black Knights. It felt as if they were testing the security boundaries around her, searching for any weakness they could use to get to her. That thought terrified her.

Fear stayed at the back of her mind no matter how hard she worked or tried to force it out.

After the incident with the electric panel, Kopack moved the classes and professors' offices to a temporary location on campus, closed the building to everyone else and wired all the windows and doors with alarms.

Still, Sassa didn't feel safe in the building. Every time she shut her eyes, she saw Chekhov marching toward her like a relentless robot.

The only way she would be truly safe was to find where Sam hid the formula because, right now, it didn't seem she would ever be able to recreate the virus and find a cure.

Frustrated, she scrubbed her hands and headed to Sam's office…although it looked less like an office and more like a nursery. Keri's toys were strewn across a blanket on the floor and right in the middle lounged broad-shouldered Officer De Luca with his long legs stretched far beyond the boundaries of the blanket. Leaning on one elbow, he stacked blocks on top of each other, which Keri promptly knocked down and laughed until she rolled over to her side.

The sound of her daughter's joyous giggles was just the medicine Sassa needed to refill her flagging spirits. She had to succeed for her daughter's sake and all the children who might die if she didn't. But first, she needed a break.

She plopped onto the couch and closed her eyes.

"I take it your latest experiment went bust." Jared had pulled Keri to a sitting position and stacked the blocks again. Peals of sweet laughter rippled across the air and Sassa smiled. She didn't answer. She didn't need to. He seemed to know what she needed.

At almost eight o'clock at night, all of her staff had left hours ago but she'd stayed on to finish. When Keri got fussy, Jared fed her a jar of baby food. The remnants still sat on the tray of the portable high chair and…now that Sassa looked…on her baby's chin.

"Thanks for taking over so I could finish." She pulled a wipe from a nearby package and cleaned the orange carrots off Keri's little round chin and the wrinkles of her chubby neck.

"You're welcome. She's fun." He frowned in bemusement, a kind of puzzled "I'm lost" look that Sassa found endearing. He gestured toward Keri's face.

"She's squirmy. I did my best to get it all."

Sassa couldn't help but chuckle at his slightly abashed tone. Who would have thought a tiny baby could fluster this big man? "You did fine. Half the time I can't tame her." She picked Keri up to give her a hug but her daughter wiggled and reached for the toys. Sassa placed her back on the blanket.

"See? You are her favorite new toy." Laughter filled her tone.

"That I can do." Dutifully, he stacked the blocks one more time. Keri pushed them over and giggled.

Sassa laughed as the baby toppled onto her side again, overcome with laughter. "She loves that little trick."

He chucked Keri's chin. "She loves tormenting me. She's a heartbreaker already."

His words struck Sassa deep and made her think of his wife. "You and your wife have no children?"

Freezing, he stared at her for a moment then slowly rose to his feet. "Ex-wife. She's my ex-wife. Our divorce was finalized, remember? And no. Thankfully, we had no children. That would have made this all the more difficult."

Sassa lowered her gaze. "Is that the reason you lost your faith? Because your marriage failed?"

Tossing the wooden block to the floor, he shook his head. "Just one more reason in a long list."

"I'm sorry. I didn't mean to pry."

He shrugged. "Partners deserve to understand each other. I grew up on a farm, just like you did. At least, for part of my life. My grandad had a place in the Coachella valley. I lived with him from the time I was eleven until I went off to college. His was the only home I ever knew. In the summertime, I'd get up before the dawn and ride the tractor with him. I loved the smell of the green, growing things. I loved watching life spring from the earth. When I went off to college, it was natural for me to go into biology." He stopped. His features had softened, as if the memories of his grandfather eased his mind. "But then, like all living things, my grandfather passed. Unfortunately for me, it was just when I needed him the most."

He looked out the office windows at the lab. "I was so lost and lonely. I needed his wisdom and his courage."

"You didn't have any other family?"

His features changed again. This time his gaze took on a shadowy, almost angry focus. "Yeah, I did. My mother. But that's another reason I'm convinced God doesn't listen. If He did, my life would have been very different."

He faced the glass again, looking away from her, but his voice still held that hard edge. "My mom was a drunk—a beautiful, helpless, dreamy girl who couldn't wait to get off the farm. She went to Hollywood determined to make it as a singer and all she found was a string of men, a bottle and me.

"We were living in a dump downtown. Hadn't eaten in days because she'd spent the last of her money on booze. She was out of her mind, gone. Someone must have called the police because they came to get us. Of course, she fought them. I was scared, yelling at them not to hurt her. This one policeman got down on my level and talked to me…just talked. I don't even remember what he said but I remember his voice. So calm and kind. The others didn't seem to care, hardly even knew I was there, but this guy never left my side…not until my grandad came to get me. His name was Petersen. Officer Petersen. I never forgot him or what he did for me. I wanted to be that kind of man so, after I got my biology degree, I went into law enforcement. Bioterrorism seemed to be the best combination of both."

"What happened to your mother?"

"Shortly after my grandfather died, the police found her on skid row in downtown LA. She was dying, too, needed hospitalization. I sold the farm to pay for her care. After she passed, I used the rest to pay for my college."

Sassa was silent for a long while. "I'm sorry."

He shook his head. "Don't be. Selling the farm didn't hurt as much as it could have. Water became too expensive. Those last few years, scrabbling a living out of the dirt killed my granddad. I didn't want to end up the same way. I wanted my life to be different, so I sold the farm and moved on."

Her heart ached for that little boy/young man caught in a world of adult problems. He had reason to be hurt and angry. She understood why he felt abandoned by God. After what she'd been through, she'd almost drowned in despair and grief. Only the grace of God and believers like her parents and Sam had helped keep her heart away from despair.

"I'm sorry you felt so alone…" She halted, almost tripping over her own words. "But later…"

Later he had a wife, someone who should have understood, should have loved and helped him overcome his difficult past. Instead, she'd turned her back on him.

Sassa looked up. Jared's gaze was focused on her, almost as if he knew exactly what she was thinking.

He gave his head a slight shake. "I don't blame Jessica for not sticking around. I disappointed her."

"I do." In point of fact, she was pretty angry with a woman she'd never met. "Ambition is never a good motive for ending a marriage, especially with a man like you who has so many other good qualities. You're a loyal friend. I've never met anyone quite so loyal. You're determined to save Sam's legacy even after he's gone. You…" She scrambled for the right words and finally just spoke her feelings out loud. "You take care of my baby like she's your own even though you don't know anything about infants. You drive an hour and a half to bring me a *hallongrotta* just to make me feel better. Friends like that are worth their weight in gold."

He shook his head, but a small smile wavered over his lips. "Jessica would say those are all things an ambitious person needs to do to get ahead…and I learned them a little too late."

"That may be why someone like Jessica does those things. But you're not like that. You're real. You're kind and caring. Besides, she gave up on you too soon. Stopping a pathogen that could destroy the world's economies is a pretty ambitious goal."

Jared shook his head. "I'm not the one who's going to save the world. You are."

"We are. Someone told me Sam chose us both."

"Not fair. You can't use my own words against me."

"I can…unless they're not true. Maybe you're wrong. Maybe *I'm* not the right person for the job."

He met her gaze, his dark brown eyes focused on her—piercing, as if they looked into her innermost being. "Yes, you are. In fact, I think you're the only one for the job."

The deep sincerity in his voice and his dark, penetrating gaze sparked something to life inside Sassa. That nebulous, tingling spark had nothing to do with confidence or certainty and everything to do with a man putting his trust in her, believing in her. She hadn't had that feeling in a long, long time. Maybe ever.

And the very last person who should be awakening that feeling was a man still in love with his wife. Because no matter how he might deny it, Sassa heard that truth beneath all his words. Jared still loved his ex-wife.

The woman didn't deserve his love. She'd let him down in ways he didn't even recognize. But that only made Sassa more determined not to let her faith in him falter. She couldn't bear to fail the grown man who stood before her, wearing his little-boy broken heart on his sleeve.

She looked away, unable to meet his unwavering gaze.

Jared touched the earpiece wrapped around his ear. Sassa tensed. It seemed like every time he did that, another Black Knights attack was in progress.

But this time Jared smiled and said, "Thanks, Butler. You're just in time." He gave her that wry grin she was beginning to recognize. The one that said he was done trying to find meaning in the world and, most of all, himself.

"We've become way too maudlin. I've got just what we need." He opened the door as an agent unlocked the outer lab door and entered, carrying two large bags. Jared met him halfway then returned. A sharp, pleasing aroma filled the small office.

Sassa's stomach rumbled. "Is that Chinese? Oh, bless you! I'm starving."

Jared set the food out on the desk. "We've got fried rice, kung pao chicken, chow mein and my personal favorite, egg foo yong. It's the best I've ever had."

Sassa paused. "From Chang's Palace on Shaw?"

Jared grinned. "You know it, too?"

"Absolutely the best. It didn't take you long to find the place."

"Hey, that's my specialty. Takeout."

Sassa laughed.

"Laugh if you must, but not all of us live in the belt of the best fresh fruits and vegetables in the country."

His words were a stark reminder for both of them of what was at stake if Sassa didn't find a cure for the pathogen. Their gazes met and fearful dread flashed between them.

"I've seen crops devastated by Xylella." His tone was low. "Row after row of dead plants. I can't imagine what this thing will do."

"I can imagine it. I can't stop the images of dead orchards and vineyards flashing through my mind. It's all I can see when I close my eyes. That and Chekhov marching toward me with that knife he used on Sam."

"We won't let him get to you, Sassa. I promise."

But it was a promise Sassa wasn't sure he could keep. Each time the Black Knights made a move, they got closer and closer. It was only a matter of time until they found a way to get to her. She and Jared looked at each other. Sassa feared her unspoken thoughts would show in her features.

She looked away first, spooned food onto her paper plate, snapped her chopsticks loose and sat on the couch. "Takeout is my staple."

Jared scooped noodles into his mouth, chewed then shook his head. "Those puréed carrots I fed Keri didn't come from the store."

"You're right about that. I try to give her the best. Once a month, I do up some fresh things for her and freeze them."

"What? Mommy doesn't deserve the best, too?"

Sassa laughed. "Mommy doesn't have time for the best—not for herself. She's too busy making it for the little girl she loves." Keri chose that moment to pull herself up on Sassa's leg. She reached for the plate on her mother's lap, but Sassa lifted it out of reach.

"From what I've seen, Mommy doesn't take the time to eat anything…not even the box of *hallongratta* she claimed she could finish."

Sassa paused. "You looked in my box of *hallongratta*? Are you checking up on me?"

Jared nodded. "Yes, I am. I told you, my partner gets what she wants. I thought you might need a refill, so I looked and saw that you hardly touched them."

She frowned. "I've been a little distracted."

"Yes, you have. But you said you're a stress eater and that's not true."

She lowered the plate to her lap. "I feel like I'm being cross-examined."

"No. I just want to point out that you say a lot of things about yourself that I'm not going to believe anymore. Especially the ones about what you *can't* do."

That unwanted tingling was back again. This time it brought a flush to her cheeks. She was glad Jared chose to focus on the plate in his hand or he would have seen the telltale blush.

That tingle was nice. Pleasant. She could get used to it if she wasn't careful.

Partners, she reminded herself. She and Jared were just partners, like he'd said. No need to get crazy over a partner. Still…it was a nice feeling. Kindness was something she didn't expect. She should return the favor and try to be a little kinder, too.

She ate the last of her egg foo yong then leaned back on the couch. Content and full, she closed her eyes. Keri chose that moment to fuss and reach for her. She pulled the baby up onto her lap, jostling the plate all the while. Leaning over, Jared took it from her hands. Keri continued to fuss and rub her eyes while Sassa cuddled her. Jared stood to throw away the plates and opened the small refrigerator behind the desk.

"Is this what she wants?" He held out a bottle.

"Told you. For someone with no children, you're pretty good."

"I'm a quick learner."

Keri settled in with the bottle, snuggling deep into her mother's arms. Sassa closed her eyes as Jared placed the leftovers in the refrigerator and gathered the empty bags. She must have dozed because she jerked awake when he placed a blanket over her and Keri.

"Oh, no. I can't fall asleep. I need to get back to work as soon as I put her in her portable crib."

Jared gently pushed her back against the pillows and crouched down to tuck the edges of the blanket around them. "You need to sleep, Sassa. You're exhausted. Tomorrow is soon enough to save the world."

A small laugh slipped out and ended in a yawn.

He was right. Sometimes she was annoyed by how right he could be. For now, though, she didn't fight him or argue. Her eyes drifted closed. He moved across the room, the lights went off and the door closed.

Why couldn't "being right" translate into "being Mr. Right"?

She nodded off before she could answer her own silly question.

FOUR

Sassa opened her eyes slowly. Murky light filtered beneath her shades, so it was later than her usual 6:00 a.m. awakening. After two more fruitless days of research and sleeping in the lab, Jared had insisted she go home for a good night's rest. After she put Keri down, she'd collapsed on her bed and slept through the night, probably because she felt safe with Jared just a shout away on her couch.

She paused. Keri should have been awake long ago. Was she as tired as her mother? She slipped from the bed and tiptoed across her wood floors to the door, hoping not to wake her sleeping child. She eased it open—just a crack—and heard the sound of Keri's giggles. Jared lay stretched out on the floor, his legs dangling off Keri's blanket again as they played their "stack the blocks and knock it over" game once more.

As she watched, her daughter lost interest and leaned forward, reaching for Jared's face. Her breath caught as her six-month-old daughter rose to her knees. This new effort made Sassa want to rush in and scoop her up, but Jared calmly held out his hands. Keri gripped his thumbs and pulled herself up...all the way to her feet. She stood on wobbly legs, grinning from ear to ear. For some reason, Sassa suppressed the urge to rush in.

"Look at you, little girl!" Jared's tone was low and so gentle, it made Sassa's heart pound. "Aren't you proud of yourself? I am. Before you know it, you'll be walking." Her legs gave way and she plopped to her well-padded bottom. Her eyes widened in surprise. Jared chuckled and that made Keri decide it was funny, too. Her sweet giggles echoed over the room.

Sassa's heart stopped.

That. That's what my baby has been missing in her life. A father who encourages, who challenges with a firm but gentle tone and makes her giggle. Tears misted her eyes and she stepped back, away from the crack in the door and leaned against the wall.

Why now, Lord? Why would you show me a perfect father now?

Of course He would show her now. What better way to open her eyes? She'd been dead set against marriage ever again. She knew Keri needed a male figure in her life, but she always believed her father would be enough. Yet the little scene she'd just witnessed told her there was more, much more, to a father. She'd been in denial…not willing to admit that Keri needed more… simply because she'd been so hurt. Erik had never showed the slightest interest in his daughter. Sassa had covered all of that hurt with attitude and anger.

But now in the dark shadows of her room, she could finally admit the truth. She wanted a father for Keri. A good man who would love her daughter like his own. She'd been struggling to get out of the morass for so long, she hadn't even dared to think of what might be possible, what hope she could have for the future.

So the Lord's timing was perfect. He'd opened her eyes and for the first time in a long time, forced her to realize what her future could look like. At least, part of it. Jared wasn't the man for her. They were opposites. They had different ideas on just about everything…what kind of houses they liked, where they should live, what success meant. Sassa had never in her life felt that success meant a high-powered job in some trend-setting town like Miami. All she'd ever wanted was a secure job in her little hometown, helping farmers keep the land that had been in their families for generations.

But if she was being truthful, Jared's arm around her at the funeral had been the only thing holding her up. Without his support, she might have fallen into a sobbing pile. He seemed to know just what she needed, when she needed it. So far, he'd been a good partner. Just like he'd suggested. Partners. That's all. Nothing more.

Good thing. The way she was feeling right now, she'd have him halfway to the altar simply because her daughter needed a father.

Sassa shook her head. Worry over the Black Knights' constant threats and frustration over her failure to figure out the formula was impacting her. She was more of an emotional mess than she realized. Marriages weren't made like that. A marriage was a promise between a man and a woman. She couldn't afford to allow other emotional responses to enter into that equation. Besides, this man was still in love with this wife!

No. The Lord had opened her eyes to the realization of her daughter's need for a father. Jared was a good partner. That's all. Wiping the tears from her eyes, she opened the door.

Jared looked up. "It's about time. We were just starting to get hungry."

"We? I didn't hear a fussy baby. In fact, all I heard was laughter."

Jared grinned. "Yeah. Me and Miss Keri have some fun, don't we?"

Keri answered by trying to stick the block in her hand into his mouth. He grasped it and shook his head. "But for the life of me, I can't figure out her fascination with my mouth."

Sassa studied his full lips and the slight five-o'clock shadow surrounding it. She understood. His mouth was pretty fascinating. She swallowed and turned away. Hadn't she just admonished herself for those kinds of thoughts?

She took a deep breath. "I think I have some eggs and bacon in the fridge. Does that sound good?"

"Sounds great. I'm starved."

Jared followed Sassa into the kitchen. He put Keri in her high chair and gave her blocks to keep her occupied. "Can I help?"

"Sure. You can make the toast. It's in the cupboard."

Jared pulled out the toaster and a bag of bread. Sassa couldn't stop the feeling that this felt normal, like a happy family. That was the last emotion she needed to have.

"I don't think we're going to have toast." Jared held up a piece of bread covered in mold.

Sassa gave a little laugh. "That's what happens when you sleep in the lab. I told you takeout is my specialty."

Jared chuckled, bundled up the bread bag and tossed it in the trash. He pulled plates out of the cupboard, shoved the files he'd been working on to a seat and set out forks. By the time he finished, the eggs and bacon were done.

Sassa set a plate in front of him. "That's the best you're going to get in this kitchen."

"And I'm happy to get it."

He lifted his fork and took a bite. Sassa slid into her seat and bowed her head. When she finished her prayer, she looked up to see him frozen, his fork halfway to his mouth.

He lowered it and shook his head. "Sorry. My manners have gotten a little rusty."

She shrugged. "Don't worry about it. Prayer is a conversation between two friends. I don't think you consider Jesus a friend."

His lips thinned and he chose not to make a comment. Part of Sassa was glad. Her comment was meant to break up their quiet little domestic scene that made her feel things she was better off not feeling.

Keri began to fuss. Sassa tested the peaches and found them soft enough to eat. She spooned the fruit into her daughter's mouth. While Sassa waited for her to chew, her gaze dropped to the pile of photos sitting on the chair beside her. In between bites, she picked the pile up and placed it on the table. She recognized the top photo of Heiser, Chekhov's right-hand man. Another photo showed a person all in black, the head and face shielded by a hoodie.

"Tell me about this guy," she said, pointing to the black hoodie. "Why is this photo so blurry? You can't even tell who it is."

"It's the only known picture of someone we suspect might be 'The Spyder'—the Black Knights' IT guy.

We don't know much about him, but we think he's very young and British. He's a legend on the dark web."

"If they don't know much about him, how do they know he's young and British?"

"His work didn't appear on the black web until about three years ago. His handiwork is pretty distinctive but untraceable. The way he programs, it seems to indicate some habits commonly taught in British schools. But we don't know anything for sure."

She held up another photo.

"Mario Rojas. Started out forging immigration papers for folks to get into the US. He branched out from there. Interpol wants him for counterfeiting money from five different countries."

She dropped the photos and spooned more fruit into Keri's mouth. "I'm sorry I asked. How did Chekhov convert all these international criminals to his cause?"

"He's passionate and committed. He chose them carefully, found people with a reason to hate. Heiser lost his whole family to a suicide bomber. Rojas rose up from the Mexico City ghetto. Each of them had lost someone or something—except Spyder. No one knows anything about him other than the fact that he's dangerous."

"All of these crazy people here in quiet central California. It's hard to believe."

"It's not only hard to believe, it's a sin. People here are just trying to live, to make every day work, sending their kids to school, planning their futures. You expect this in LA or…"

"Miami?"

Jared studied her, his dark eyes reaching deep inside, like he was so capable of doing. "You remembered I wanted to be stationed there. Yes, I guess you'd expect this kind of activity in Miami but not here. It's so peaceful, so…comfortable."

"You almost sound like you like my hometown."

"I like what it represents. A rich heritage. Good families. Hardworking men and women doing their best, struggling day after day to do right. No one knows better than me how easily someone can fall off that hard road. It happened to my mother."

They were both silent. Jared obviously lost in his memories, and Sassa…her heart bleeding for the little boy Jared had once been…the one she couldn't help, hold or even love. At last, a thought came to her.

"There's one thing to learn from all of this, Jared. It just proves that your skills are needed everywhere. I hope you remember that in the future."

Surprise filtered through his features. Did he understand what she meant? That Jared was the right man for the job, too, just like his grandfather had said?

After a moment, he nodded. "I'll remember. And I promise you, I'm going to do my best to find them. These men don't belong here and I'm going to see that they don't 'belong' anywhere."

Voices rose in the other room. Seated at Sam's desk, Jared looked out the window of the office. Sassa and Sam's lab assistant exchanged words. The encounter was not heated. In fact, Matt put an arm around Sassa and gave her a one-armed hug. Probably one of encouragement.

Sassa still had no breakthrough in her research. The strain was beginning to wear her down. The Black Knights had not stopped their constant distractions.

A student rally outside the lab building almost developed into a riot.

After several tense hours, campus security was able to break it up, but they could not determine who started the fight or even trace the organizers of the rally.

Jared knew exactly who the mysterious organizers were and so did Sassa.

Fear and frustration were apparent in her body movements, and especially in her permanently clouded features. Her brilliant mind seemed to be churning continuously. Often, Jared would see a look of concentration on her face and she would be miles away, silently turning equations over and over again.

He wished he could help. He tried, even sent Sam's ID bracelet to a jeweler to have several links removed so Sassa could wear it. She was very thankful and never took it off, but strain was still evident in her every move.

She'd hardly eaten in the last two weeks. He suspected she'd lost weight. Her cheeks had a gaunt look that hadn't been there before. The only time she lost that haunted look was when she held Keri. But even then, she'd touch the baby's face, trace a finger down her cheek like she was trying to memorize it. Jared could almost sense her thoughts running to the children who would suffer if she didn't find the equation for the pathogen.

He paused. Was that where her occasionally snarky comments came from? A truly sensitive heart trying to protect itself?

Jared suspected that was true. One thing he knew for sure. Every strong emotion she had was reflected in her features. Frustration. Fear. Love. Empathy. Anyone who looked at Sassa knew what she was feeling.

So different from Jessica, who hid her emotions behind a cool, aloof wall of no response. Frankly, he'd rather face Sassa's snarky comments than Jessica's cold wall. At least he knew where he stood with Sassa. With Jessica, he was always guessing. Always trying to figure out what he did wrong.

He stopped. He hadn't thought of Jessica in days. And now he waited for the wave of hurt and sadness that usually swept over him.

It didn't happen. He took a deep breath of surprise. Perhaps he was finally beginning to heal. Or maybe he had more important things on his mind than his failed marriage…like trying to be a good partner to a woman on the edge.

One change he'd noticed: some of Sassa's snark was gone. He wasn't sure exactly when she'd dropped that protective mechanism. It seemed to fade away as she began to trust him. And she did trust him. He'd worked hard to earn her faith and he intended to live up to her expectations. At least, that was the plan…which brought him back to the file in his hand.

He'd read and reread the report on Jacob Heiser for the sixth time, hoping he'd catch some hint, some clue, as to the man's weakness. He found nothing. Heiser's planned attacks were nearly faultless. In fact, the only clue they had to most of his suspected crimes was that they had been executed flawlessly, like the incident at the airport. Jared was certain Heiser was behind the bomb scare that distracted Kopack's team, leaving a minimal guard on Sam.

Glass shattered and Jared looked up to see Sassa standing in the middle of the floor, her hands in the air like she'd dropped something. He set the photo down and hurried out. Matt and two of the other lab assistants had already reached Sassa by the time he did. She stood for a long while, not moving, her eyes closed, while they began to sweep up the shards of glass.

When Jared touched her arm, she took a deep breath and gave him a rueful smile. "Imagine what would have happened if that tray had been full of viruses."

He glanced down at the shattered empty vials and looked up. The smile had faded.

"Sam insisted on everyone being well rested and calm when they entered the lab. He always said, 'leave the world's troubles at the door.'" She shook her head. "I don't think he took into account that the world might be waiting just outside that door, depending on me."

She was close to tears. No matter how hard she tried to hide it, Jared knew it was true. He glanced at his watch. "It's 4:00 p.m. Time to call it a day. Matt and the others can finish this. Let's go get Keri and have an early dinner."

She shook her head, but Matt took her hand. "Let us finish, Sassa. We can handle this. Go home. Get some sleep. We'll start fresh tomorrow."

Finally, with four heads bobbing in agreement, she capitulated. Smiling, she said, "You all just want me out of here so you can stop cleaning up my messes."

Matt smiled. "How did you guess?"

Sassa chuckled. Jared was extremely glad to hear the sound. She needed to let go, even if it was just for a few hours. He'd order pizza to be delivered and maybe play some old movies. Sam had once told him she loved old black-and-white films. He'd stream four old slapstick comedies, and make her sit through all of them.

He helped her out of her lab coat and handed it to Matt. Then they gathered their things from the office and drove across campus to pick up little Keri.

Jared's step was lighter as they stepped out of the SUV. Frankly, a night of old movies sounded very good to him. He wasn't usually one for that type of entertainment, but right now it sounded pretty close to perfect.

A crowd was gathered in front of the child-care center.

"Oh, no." Jared barely heard Sassa's murmured words, but they matched the pounding in his heart.

He reached for her hand. "I'm sure it's all right. Keri's guard is with her."

Pulling her forward, they jogged to the crowd and pushed their way through. Agent Edwards, Keri's guard, stood just outside the fragmented front window of the center.

Jared's pulse picked up another notch. "Edwards! What happened?"

"Someone threw a brick through it. I've called for backup and campus security. They should be here any minute."

"Where's Keri?"

"In the backyard. Fortunately, this is past the usual pickup time for most of the children. The few remaining ones were in the back, so no one was hurt."

Usual time… The children still here were in the back…

It was a diversion tactic. Heiser's usual ploy.

"Keri!"

Dropping Sassa's hand, Jared spun and ran through the front door. Near the entrance, across from the broken window, was a check-in desk. Jared ran past to the large playroom. This main area opened onto the backyard. Jared dodged piles of toys and a low, small shelving unit.

Jared recognized one of the center's workers. She stood just outside the sliding-glass door, holding Keri in her arms and talking to a toddler. Her gaze was focused on the youngster at her feet. Behind her, at the back of the large yard, Jared saw a man's head pop up as he climbed over the brick fence. Strapped to his back was an empty child carrier.

Heiser! And he was headed straight for Keri!

The young worker looked up. Obviously remembering Jared from previous visits, she started to wave as he leaped over buckets of toys, kicked a small scooter, tripped and stumbled, but managed to keep his feet.

When he looked up, the young woman's smile of greeting had faded and she stared at him, a puzzled expression on her features. Behind her, Heiser was over the fence and pulling a long knife out of a sheath attached to his leg. He strode toward the unsuspecting worker. He was going to attack the poor young woman!

Jared shouted. His voice was muffled through the door, but the young woman turned. Jared pulled out his gun and slammed open the sliding door so hard, it bumped against the side and bounced back.

They young worker turned, screamed and stumbled away, cradling Keri and dragging the young toddler with her. Jared aimed his gun at Heiser and steadied it with his other hand. Another worker shouted and began to herd the children toward the door.

With Heiser's quarry so close to the door and Jared standing between them, he sheathed his knife and spun, running back to the fence he'd just climbed.

Relieved he didn't have to use his gun around the children, Jared shoved it back in the holster.

"More officers are on the way," he shouted to the workers. "Get these children inside and lock the door behind you."

They both nodded and Jared ran for the fence. It took him two leaps to get his long legs over the top, but Heiser had done it in one. For a moment, he wondered what he was doing chasing after a professional killer in such good shape. But only for a moment.

The man had threatened Keri. He was going after him no matter what.

Jared rolled over the top of the fence and landed on his feet. Heiser was running down the campus sidewalk, along a small interior road meant only for carts. Heiser had planned his escape route ahead of time. No police or security vehicles would reach them on that path. If Jared was going to catch him, it would have to be on foot. He lunged into a run and followed the killer.

Jared had refused to let his desk job bog him down, so he'd established a strong, solid workout routine and maintained it for years. But apparently it wasn't the same caliber of training as Heiser's. The man moved like a sleek cat. Fortunately, Jared had long legs and was a good runner.

Suddenly, Heiser made a sharp turn, leaped over a small cement divider and ran straight through the middle of a group of students, shoving as he went. One young woman fell to the ground. Several of her fellow students shouted and two young men started after Heiser.

Jared shouted. "Stay out of the way!" But his shout

was too late. He lost precious minutes as he dodged around the startled, angry group.

"Call the campus police. Tell them where we are."

One young woman was already on her phone. Jared saw her nod as he passed. He'd lost ground on Heiser and had to turn up the speed.

The man dodged in and out of a temporary, standing art exhibit. For a moment, Jared thought he'd lost him, but then he appeared at the edge of the clearing, headed for some buildings. If he got inside, Jared would lose him for sure. He sped up.

Workout or not... I can't keep this up much longer.

In the distance he heard the whine of sirens. Thankfully, they were close. Heiser heard them, too, because he paused. Once again, he changed direction, made an immediate ninety-degree right turn, and disappeared around the corner.

Not sure what might be waiting for him, Jared slowed. Unholstering his gun, he edged out until he could see around the building. Heiser was not lying in wait. He had run ahead of Jared about fifty feet, toward another cluster of buildings that looked like dorms. A rabbit warren of rooms in which to get lost.

Taking a deep breath, Jared holstered his gun and began to run again.

Heiser had to cross a main thoroughfare to get to the dorms. Men ran from opposite ends of the road, converging on the large common area divided only by the street. Apparently, Kopack's men and the campus police had determined Heiser's escape route and followed. They ran, yelling and clearing pedestrians out of the way. But cars continued to shoot across the street. Jared came to the curb and waited for two to pass. Heiser had only one escape route...straight ahead.

Heiser jogged a step before he stopped short. Another group of security men and police appeared from between the buildings in front of him.

The assassin was trapped. Jared drew his gun, his gaze fixed on Heiser. Across the street, the assassin looked at him, gave him a mock salute then stepped right in front of an oncoming municipal bus.

Jared shouted. The bus screeched to a stop. But not soon enough.

Sassa stood to the side of the check-in desk, clutching Keri as close as she could. A female professor Sassa knew snatched up her three-year-old before saying a few quiet words to Julie, the director of the child-care center. Spinning, she gave Sassa a silent, icy glare.

Sassa didn't blame her. Her daughter's presence here in the center had endangered innocent children, a calamity she wouldn't allow to happen again. Keri wouldn't return to the center until this was over.

Still, the fearful and angry glances from some of the parents hurt. They struck down deep, to an old hurt.

Sassa had once been the ideal teenager, the one who would go far. The whole small town of Kingsburg had been behind her, cheering her on, taking pride in her success as if it were their own. Their pride had made her downfall even more difficult. The disappointment and discouragement she'd seen in their faces had doubled her own feelings of failure. The angry look of her coworker brought all those feelings back.

Keri wiggled in her arms and rubbed her eyes. It was close to her dinnertime and she needed a diaper change. Her skin was also a little hot to the touch. Was that tooth bothering her again?

Sassa bounced her in her arms, trying to soothe her, and glanced at the door. Jared still wasn't back. Why hadn't he returned? What if he was hurt?

Her heart started pounding and she spun to face the back door and the fence he'd disappeared over. She closed her eyes.

Please, Lord. Don't let anything happen to him. I need him.

Her eyes flew open. How was it that she had come to rely on another man? How had she let that happen?

Keri whimpered again. Sassa felt like whimpering, too.

She had fallen hard for Erik, the popular, fun-loving boy everyone adored. It hadn't mattered to her that he had no faith life or even that he had little respect for hers. She had no idea how much it would come to matter or that Erik couldn't live without that adoration. In fact, he craved the attention that came from being attached to the most popular girl in town. He craved it more than his love for her and their soon-to-be-born child. But when the attention disappeared, and the hard work of married life began, Erik had fallen apart. It wasn't long before he'd gone in search of the attention he needed. He found it in bars and casinos.

The stress of their life had caused Sassa to lose their child. Shortly after, Erik ran away, headed to Las Vegas and new territory. Sassa went back to school, determined to get on with her life. But Erik came back, begging her to forgive him.

She gave him a second chance. After all, it was her Christian duty, right? Besides, she still loved him. Or rather, she loved the man she knew he *could* be if he followed the Lord's path for him. She felt she owed it to that man to give him a second chance at life.

For a while, things had gone well. They had the marriage Sassa had always dreamed of, but soon, she recognized the signs of restlessness. The need to be adored returned. Sassa realized her love for Erik would never satisfy that need. It would never be enough. Only the Lord could satisfy that kind of bone-deep need and Erik refused to turn to Him.

One morning, she'd woken up and Erik was gone. Her bank account had been emptied and she was pregnant with Keri. She'd given up the childish wish of a happily-ever-after and clung to the Lord. It was inconceivable to her now that she'd become dependent on another man, another man who couldn't place his life in the hands of God.

But Jared was just a friend, the partner she needed in this desperate situation. She wasn't—wouldn't fall in love. He'd been so much help to her, always by her side, anticipating her needs, and lifting her up when she was down. He'd promised her they would be great partners and he was right. She'd never had a friend like him, let alone a partner, and these were extraordinary circumstances. She needed all the help she could get. There was nothing wrong with needing a good friend in this intense situation.

She bounced her daughter and shifted her to her other arm just as the last parent picked up their child and left. The director of the child-care center walked toward her. Julie and Sassa had started working for the university about the same time. They were both single moms and had developed a bond. Now Julie's face was wreathed in worry.

Sassa lifted her hand. "You don't need to say anything, Julie. I completely understand, and I'm so sorry."

Julie grasped her hand in both of hers. "Don't apologize. How could you know? But I have to protect the other children."

"Of course. I understand completely."

Julie squeezed her hand. "What will you do?"

Sassa took a deep breath. "Try to survive."

"Don't say that!"

Her friend's heartfelt cry moved Sassa. Tears blurred her vision, but she blinked them away. "It's all right, Julie. Really. I have wonderful protection. You saw what happened. They'll take good care of me."

She sounded convinced…more convinced than she felt. Her world kept shattering, piece by piece. Safe place by safe place. Was there no stopping the Black Knights?

Just when she felt her strength and her convictions slipping, the front door opened. Jared came through, followed by Kopack and other agents. She was so relieved, she hurried toward them. Jared spied her across the room and moved to her in two long strides. He reached her and pulled her into his arms. Startled, she looked up. He wore an expression she couldn't define. Was it fear or shock? Maybe both.

Filled with trepidation, Sassa leaned into him. "What is it? What happened?"

"He walked in front of a bus, Sassa. Heiser stepped in front so he wouldn't be captured. I was right across the street and I couldn't stop him. No one could."

Horror was written in his features. Heiser's actions

had struck him to the core. Tension rippled through his body, making it stiff.

"You can't blame yourself, Jared. You did all you could to stop him."

He shook his head. "That's what worries me." He pulled her closer, tucked her beneath his chin and whispered, "We can't stop them. They're killing themselves to serve their cause, Sassa. How can we protect you and Keri from that kind of madness?"

The tautness in his body was for her and Keri? Did he really care that much? Looking up, she met his gaze. Something in his brown eyes, a tenderness she hadn't seen before, warmed her. It melted all of her fear. In his arms, she felt safe, sure that he would protect them. Madness could not stand against what she saw in that look.

She wrapped her arms around his waist and leaned into him, pressing her cheek against his chest. She could hear the hard pounding of his strong heart. A heart like that would stop at nothing. Right now, she was certain it beat for her.

Jared ducked his head and buried his face in her hair. He kissed the top of her head and held her close. Everything inside her shattering world stilled. All at once, life balanced and righted itself.

It would be all right. They would succeed. Together they could do it.

Keri whimpered again and wiggled against Jared's tight hold. Jared lifted her into one arm but kept his other around Sassa. That strong arm was around her daughter, holding and cherishing the most precious thing in her life. And one more hard thing inside her melted. She felt nothing but certainty.

"Come on. Let's get you and Keri home where it's quiet."

He guided her over to Kopack, deep in discussion with his second-in-command. Jared marched up to the man with a purposeful determination. "I'm taking Sassa back to the lab. We need to regroup before we do anything else and I think you need to double her guard. I want two more men with her at all times."

Agent Kopack looked up with frowning features. "I'm not sure we have two men to spare."

"Then find them. I'll get some special agents sent out here from the border patrol. Or better yet, get some municipal officers. They know the area best. We need their knowledge."

Sassa eyed Jared as he stood up to Kopack. At first, the agent seemed irritated by Jared's commanding tone. So far, Jared had deferred to the lead FBI agent. This new, demanding Jared startled them both. Kopack seemed to resent it. Sassa loved it.

The only people who'd ever stood up for her were Sam and her parents. Having this man do it, a man like Jared, made something open inside her. That feeling bloomed like a flower.

After a long while, Kopack's frown disappeared. "You're right, De Luca. We need more men. The Black Knights are determined to accomplish their goal or die in the effort. We won't forget that again. I'll see about getting more local and county police involved. Send for your extra agents. We need all the help we can get."

Jared nodded and started to turn with Sassa still tucked in his arm. Kopack stopped them. "By the way, De Luca, I appreciate how you handled yourself a while ago. That was quick thinking. If you hadn't stopped

Heiser, he would have taken the baby. I may have said a few things earlier…" He paused. "Anyway, I'm glad you're on the team. I won't forget that in my report to Washington."

Jared's reaction to Kopack's comment was so strong, Sassa felt it. The tension eased out of Jared's body and a pleased grin swept over his features. That grin made Sassa's heart drop to her toes. Kopack's compliment meant a great deal to him. Too much!

Of course it meant a lot. A positive report to Washington could put Jared on course for the high-profile job he craved. Kopack's good opinion meant everything. Sassa and Keri were incidentals, the means to an end…a job well done that would put Jared on the fast track to his dream.

Everything that moments ago had blossomed inside her wilted.

All Jared's knowing looks, the half smiles of understanding, the concern, the protection, the nice words about partnerships and working well together had created a hope inside her…a hope that was bound to disappoint. Hadn't she learned that with Erik? Wasn't that the lesson she vowed never to forget? And yet, here she was, half in love with another man who had no faith in God and dreams and ambitions beyond the simple life she desired. Because no matter how kind and thoughtful Jared seemed right now, eventually his needs would outweigh hers and they would carry him away. The need to succeed, that ever-reaching desire, was greater than anything else in his life. She and Keri could never compete.

She had to remember that, had to put a stop to all

the foolish emotions trying to come to life inside her. Right here. Right now.

Reaching up, she pulled Keri into her arms and slipped away from Jared. She grabbed the diaper bag from behind the counter and headed for the door.

Jared was close behind but she didn't slow or wait. She marched out the door, her armor back in place.

She wouldn't forget again. There could be no partnership…no safety tucked beneath his arm. Ever.

FIVE

Jared stood to one side of the lab table watching Sassa and her three assistants work an experiment. Wearing her lab coat and protective eyewear, Sassa carefully inserted her hands into the gloves of the sealed, glass container. After the close call with Keri, they'd returned to the lab and Sassa had opted to get back to work instead of taking the evening off. The old, driven Sassa had returned. Determination filled every muscle in her body, so much so, she even moved as if her muscles were rigid.

At first Jared thought the threat to Keri had renewed her protective senses. But as time wore on and she refused to allow him to help with the infant, he knew something else was wrong. She'd built the wall between them again…just when he thought they were beginning to trust each other. So what happened? Was it the kiss?

He hadn't meant anything by it. It was simply an honest, emotional response to his experience. Rage had carried him across the campus in his chase after Heiser… until the man had stepped in front of the bus.

The smile of victory he'd shot Jared just before the bus hit, still haunted him. Only then did he remember he was chasing a madman driven to stop at nothing. Jared had returned to the child-care center, shaking inside, not only with awareness but relief. If Heiser had reached Keri…

Even now Jared shivered thinking of it. The kiss he gave Sassa was born of shock, thankfulness and relief. Nothing else. Surely she knew that?

He admired Sassa. She was an amazing mother. The life she was trying to provide for her daughter was a good one. Jared wished he'd had that kind of life with his mother. If his mom had half of Sassa's determination and work ethic, they might have made it.

He also understood Sassa's determination to stand on her own two feet. How many times had his grandfather stepped in to bail them out? His mom had never seen it as a hand up for Jared's benefit. Instead, she used it as a crutch to continue living the life she chose…until she drowned in a cesspit of her own making.

Sassa would never let that happen to Keri. Never. And Jared would never do anything to interfere, harm or stand in the way of that purpose. He only wanted Sassa to survive so she could succeed…so they could both succeed. Was that so wrong?

Of course, he found her attractive. She bemoaned her curves but they made her soft and womanly, took all the sharp edges off. Some men might be intimidated by her brains, but he found intelligent women endlessly fascinating. He'd married one. Jessica was intelligent and strong. He waited for the cringe of pain that came every time he thought of Jessica. But it didn't come.

I am healing. Or maybe a petite blonde with fierce strength and an occasionally caustic mouth has something to do with it.

Certainly, since he'd met Sassa, he'd learned a woman could have an amazing career and be an amazing mother, too. It took strength and hard work, but some women could do it. Maybe Jessica had known all along that she didn't have that kind of courage. That's why she'd chosen the path she had, the easy one without children and without him.

That thought made him even more determined to help Sassa…if she'd allow it.

For two long days after Keri's attempted kidnapping, Sassa wouldn't let him help with the baby, even when she was her most fussy…and she'd done a lot of fussing. Sassa said she was getting a new tooth and just needed her mother. So last night, as he'd watched from his cot through the glass partition of Sam's office, Sassa had juggled and rocked Keri in her arms, clacking away at the computer with one hand. She hadn't turned off the lights until very late. Then early, before daylight, she was up. The computer screen's bluish glow over the lab had woken him. Obviously, she'd come up with a new idea because as soon as Keri went down for her morning nap, Sassa had the assistants preparing a new test.

Now he watched as she carefully dropped a chemical onto a clear plate of glass and waited. No one around the table moved. All four pairs of eyes were fixed on the tiny plate. The tension in their features sent anticipation rushing through Jared. His muscles tightened… just as Keri began to fuss.

Sassa shot him a frustrated look. Jared simply nodded and rushed to the office. The baby had pushed herself into a sitting position and was rubbing her eyes. The minute she saw Jared, her little arms reached for him and her little lips puckered.

A rush of affection flowed through him. He'd committed himself to protecting Sassa and Keri for Sam's sake. But now that he knew them, now that he'd held little Keri in his arms, he could not imagine going on with his life if he failed them. Saving Sassa and Keri had become more important to him than his own life. His white-hot rage when he chased Heiser had proved that.

Please...if anything happens to them... Jared's words faded off into nothingness.

Funny. Those thoughts started out sounding like a prayer. He hadn't prayed in years. But before every meal and at bedtime, Sassa paused and prayed out loud with Keri. Those moments must have brought back memories of his grandfather's plain words and fierce faith. He'd been such a prayer warrior.

But all Grandad's words and faith hadn't saved his daughter.

Jared wished it had happened. Wished his grandfather's sincere belief could have saved his mother. When he was young, he'd wished and prayed for it with all his heart. At times, he'd felt that someone was out there... listening. But those feelings had faded. His grandfather died, then his mother. His prayers and the hope of someone listening died, too.

He'd lost the farm but finished college with a new goal, a new purpose. A deep, secret hope that the sacred vows he'd made to Jessica would hold their marriage together. But there had been nothing sacred in them and even that last hope had died.

He wished he was wrong. Wished there was a great and powerful God whose strength he could draw on because he needed it. Even with all the precautions Kopack and his men had taken, the Black Knights still found ways to get close to Sassa and Keri. Fear clamped his stomach like a vise, causing him to clutch Keri tighter.

She whimpered and he immediately loosened his hold. "I'm sorry, baby."

Keri nestled her face into the curve of his neck with a small sound. "What's the matter, sweetheart? Is that tooth hurting you?" The sweet baby smell, one he'd come to love, swept over him. She whimpered again and he pressed his lips into her blond curls, much in the same way he'd kissed her mother.

"See? It's just a gesture of affection. But how can we convince Mommy?"

Keri looked up at him, her big blue eyes rimmed with tears. He cupped the back of her head and kissed her again. "You really don't feel well, do you? It's all right. Mommy will be here in a minute."

In fact, Sassa had already pulled her hands out of the sealed gloves in the container and was jerking her lab coat off in a frustrated manner. She strode to the office. But instead of taking Keri from his arms, she marched to the full trash can and began digging through the crumpled papers near the top. Sassa's assistants usually shredded all the papers in the lab, but they hadn't had time for that task this morning. As soon as they'd arrived, Sassa had started the now "failed" experiment.

Sassa grabbed the top paper, carefully unfolded it, then tossed it to the floor beside the metal can. She grasped the next one.

After a few puzzled moments, Jared said, "I take it the experiment was a failure."

She pulled out another paper, smoothed it and glanced across it. "Yes. Something's wrong."

Another paper joined the ones on the floor. Jared

waited for her to finish her explanation but instead, she lifted the paper. "This is the one."

Jared joined her and scanned the scribbled equations on the page. "What is it?"

"This is the scratch note I made last night before I entered the formula into the computer. I was certain I had found the answer." She slid into the desk chair and brought up the computer screen. Keri squirmed, reaching for her mother. Jared shifted her to the other arm, hoping the baby wouldn't distract Sassa from her train of thought.

Formulas appeared on the screen, along with instructions Sassa had typed for the experiment. She held the paper up to the screen and compared the two equations. "There! There's the discrepancy. The computer formula I used for the experiment is missing a decimal."

She looked at Jared expectantly.

He frowned. "You worked very late last night, Sassa. You can't be upset with yourself for dropping a decimal."

"You don't understand. I didn't drop it. I held my notes up to the screen just like this and compared them. Not once, Jared, but three times. I've been having trouble with my formulas. I've had to check and recheck them due to lots of errors. I'd chalked those mistakes up to stress and exhaustion. But last night I knew I was tired and couldn't afford to make an error."

He stared at her. "You're saying...someone's been tampering with the formulas on the computer? Why would they do that? Besides, that's impossible. The IT guys have been monitoring your computer. They'd know if someone had accessed it."

"It's easy enough to find out. I'll check my files to

see who logged in last." She shifted back to the keyboard.

"Wait. Don't do anything." His mind was whirling.
"If someone has mirrored your screen and you look up
that data record, they'll know we suspect a problem."

She froze. "What should I do?"

"Don't do anything." He handed her Keri, pulled his
cell phone out of his pocket and dialed his supervisor in
Washington. The phone rang and rang, so he hung up
and dialed an emergency number. Someone came on
the line immediately and transferred him to the border
patrol's IT department. Much to his relief, the IT man
in charge of the combined FBI and border patrol team's
efforts answered the call. Mark was a friend of Jared's
and he quickly explained the situation.

"Give me a few minutes and I'll get back to you."
Mark hung up and Jared lowered his phone.

Sassa stared at him. Her eyes, so much like her
daughter's, looked wide, innocent and frightened. "What
did they say?"

Jared shook his head. "We had a piece of good for-
tune. Mark is the IT specialist on duty. I've talked to
him quite a bit since this started. He knows Spyder's
techniques and trademarks better than anyone. That's
why they put him in charge of the team. But the Spyder
knows Mark, too. They're like dueling hackers. Mark
says that the Spyder is the only one he knows who is
capable of creating a program to bypass the security he
designed. Mark thought he was on top of everything.
He's pretty upset that the Spyder might have gotten
past him."

She closed her eyes. "If Mark believes the Spyder got
through his security, then the hacker has the formula."

Jared's blood turned cold. "What makes you so sure?"

"I'm almost positive the formula I worked out last night is the correct one. That's why I was so frustrated when the experiment failed just now. I knew something was wrong, so I came in here to double-check my work."

"Why would Spyder access the file, copy it and then alter it? It doesn't make sense."

"Mark told you Spyder likes to play games. Maybe he's been toying with me."

"You think he's been trying to throw you off by tampering with your numbers?" Jared asked.

Sassa nodded, her eyes wide. "Maybe he's been stalling my efforts, trying to give Chekhov the time he needs to find Sam's formula. Or, more important, the time he needs to get to me. The last thing the Black Knights want is for me to discover the formula and share it with your scientists at the border patrol. As soon as that happens, they'll start on a cure. Even if Chekhov finds Sam's copy of the formula, a cure would destroy his plan."

"You may be right. Chekhov would work both angles—find Sam's copy and get to you at the same time."

Jared's phone rang. "Tell me you have good news for me."

"I'm afraid not." Mark's tone was intense. "It looks like there might be another open link to her computer, but because it's inactive I can't say for sure. Have Ms. Nilsson start typing. I'll send a ping through to see if it lasts longer or goes farther than usual. I might even be able to follow the ping to its location."

"Hang on." He turned to Sassa. "Don't you usually write a report after an experiment?"

"Yes."

"Start one now. Don't say anything about discovering the mistake in the formula. Just say the experiment was a failure." He reached for Keri and fumbled with his phone, almost dropping it before he switched on the speaker so Sassa could hear. Then he tucked the baby into the crook of his arm.

With her arms free, Sassa paused for a moment then began to type.

Jared spoke into the phone. "She's typing, Mark."

"Got it. I'll send the ping along the line."

They waited. Keri squirmed in his arms and fussed as Sassa typed furiously. Jared held his breath.

At last, Mark spoke. "I've got it! A location." He rattled off an address.

Sassa nodded. "That sounds like downtown Fresno."

Mark heard her response. "Should I send the address to Kopack and the team?"

"No. If Spyder hacked our computer system, he may also have hacked our communications. I'll contact Kopack from this end. In the meantime, do your best to make sure the Spyder doesn't know we've found him."

"Will do."

Jared hung up then studied Sassa's scratch paper, trying to memorize the equation. He looked up and met her worried gaze. "Maybe we can move fast enough to get your formula back."

Kopack assembled a team with the speed and silence that amazed Jared. Local police units met them halfway, lights flashing but sirens silent. Some of the one-way streets at the center of town were already cordoned off when they arrived. Kopack and Jared climbed out of their vehicle and met near the front of the building.

Kopack studied him. "I don't need to ask if you can handle this." His words sent warmth shooting through Jared. He didn't need Kopack's approval to do his job. But knowing that he was an equal part of the team filled a hole. That thought eased him in ways he didn't expect. It felt good to feel worthy and capable. It gave him the shot of adrenaline he needed in this situation.

"We've decided to let the local police take the lead on the breach. They know the area better…especially this building. The chief tells me this apartment building is a known haven for criminals. Our team will stand back and cover any escape. I want you far away from any confrontations because as soon as we have our hands on his computer, I want you to check for the formula and if he sent the info to someone else. Am I clear?"

"Loud and clear."

Kopack strode forward and greeted the chief of police. The man nodded. "Your suspect is in there. My men spoke with the building supervisor. To our surprise, he cooperated. Seems like he's a little worried about your suspect. Says there's lots of electronic equipment hooked up in the apartment. It has overloaded the system twice and the manager had some encounters with your character. Sounds like the suspect put the heebie-jeebies in the apartment manager. 'Freaked him' in his words. One other thing. Your suspect is a woman."

Jared and Kopack halted their movements.

The police chief studied them, his gaze moving from Kopack to Jared and back. "So you didn't know. The manager confirmed it. Says she's tiny but vicious.

Seems she threatened him with multiple ways to hurt him if he interrupted her again."

Kopack took a deep breath. "He's right. This woman is dangerous. She will not hesitate to take down your men, so tell them to be extra cautious." The chief nodded and turned away to speak into the radio attached to his shoulder.

Jared shook his head. Just when he thought they were gaining on the Black Knights, they found some new and shocking way of upsetting them. The Spyder was a woman. Jared pulled out his phone and texted the info to his IT team in Washington. No matter what happened, he wanted Mark to have this additional information. If she escaped…

Jared didn't have the time to finish his thought. The police chief gave the signal and men in SWAT uniforms entered the building. They operated as a single, efficient unit that impressed Jared. Within minutes they had the lobby cleared and were signaling for Kopack's team to enter.

The team didn't use the ramshackle elevator. Jared was glad—it looked as if it hadn't been serviced in years. The SWAT team signaled again and Jared followed up the stairs. On the third floor of the four-floor apartment building, the SWAT team signaled for Kopack's men to hold back. They halted in the stairwell as the SWAT team exited and closed the door behind them.

For one long moment—silence. Then a boom echoed through the building as the police breached the door and entered the apartment. Shouts of "This is the police!" echoed through the door, but further words were muffled as they moved deeper into the apartment. Then another loud stretch of silence had Jared holding his breath again.

At last, a SWAT officer opened the door. "The apartment is empty. Looks like your suspect got away."

Kopack made a harsh sound then looked at Jared. "Wait here."

He signaled his men forward and left Jared. Frustration made his blood pound. His senses tingled. Sound seemed amplified in the empty stairwell. He heard a small click and then a soft swish from above. Looking up, he saw a slender figure lean over the stairwell then jerk back. Running footsteps echoed away from him.

He pulled the door open and shouted, "She's here!" then spun and lunged up the steps to the roof.

One flight up, he paused at the door, heart pounding even louder. He inched the door open, expecting a bullet to come whizzing toward him. When nothing happened, he opened it farther and peeked around both corners. Directly in front of him was the large metal box of the air-conditioning unit. He couldn't see around it, but a scan of the immediate area assured him the Spyder was not on this side of the roof.

Taking a deep breath, he stepped out and hurried to the other side of the box. Easing out, he scanned the roof. A slender woman in the typical black pants and T-shirt of the Black Knights ran from one end of the roof to the other. Her long black hair flew in the wind as she searched for a way down.

Jared eased away from the unit. She was standing at the edge of the roof, looking down. As he watched, she stepped up onto the edge.

Immediately, Heiser's gloating grin as he stepped in

front of the bus popped into Jared's mind. The Spyder
was going to jump.

No! Not this time!

Jared lunged for her. The wind whistled around
him…around them both. Between the wind swirling
around the roof and Spyder's intense focus, she didn't
hear him until he was only a foot or two away. Startled,
she took a step forward. Jared dove for her, wrapped his
arm around her waist and caught her midair. He out-
weighed her by a hundred pounds and his heavier mo-
mentum carried them both sideways onto the safety of
the roof. They rolled over and over. Even before they
stopped, Spyder kicked and punched at him. She aimed
the flat of her hand at his nose. She meant to break it,
but Jared turned his head and her palm smashed against
his cheek. It hurt, but not as much as a blow to the nose
would have.

He grunted but held tight. Suddenly she shifted. Her
hands were no longer punching at his face, searching to
do damage. They lay on their sides, facing each other.
He started to tighten his hold. Almost too late, he realized she was reaching for the gun on the ground beside
them. He grasped her wrist but she wriggled the other
hand free. Jared pushed with his legs and rolled on top
of her, pinning her arm beneath both their bodies. With
his greater weight, he was able to hold her down as Kopack and his team burst out of the door and onto the
roof. Even then, the Spyder didn't give up.

Her head lunged forward and, like a vicious animal,
she tried to bite Jared's face. Two men grasped her arms.
Jared rolled free as they dragged her back, still spitting
and struggling to reach the edge of the roof.

Kopack helped Jared to his feet but he never took

his gaze off her face. Her features were twisted into a mask of boiling rage.

Heiser's mocking smile of defiance. The Spyder's rage. How many others in the Black Knights were poised on the brink of uncontrollable emotions? How could they possibly defeat such violent hatred?

Lord, help us.

Sassa finished her fake report but was afraid to close her computer until she heard from Jared. She rose and began to pace, wondering what was going on.

Did they catch the hacker? Did he have the file with the formula? Had she finally discovered the right one, the formula Sam had stumbled upon months ago?

She couldn't sit still or stop her mind from churning with questions. Sassa had to do something. Hitching her daughter onto her hip, she headed out of the small office and straight for the door. She cracked it open and met Agent Paulsen's puzzled gaze.

"Any word yet?"

"No, ma'am. I'll let you know if I hear something."

She nodded and shut the door. Matt and the other lab assistants, Libby and Jacki, had just finished cleaning up the last experiment.

Matt paused. "All done. Do you want me to close up?"

Sassa shook her head. "Set it up for one more test. Libby, will you take Keri for me?"

The assistants exchanged looks.

Sassa read the frustration in their features. "I know it's late, but we have to try one more time. I think this is the one."

Matt hesitated, but only for a moment. "All right. One more time…for Sam."

Sassa smiled. "For Sam."

Libby reached for the glass slides. "Let me get these set up and I'll take little Miss Keri."

Matt went to the cabinet where they kept the specimens and Jacki, the youngest of the lab assistants, shrugged. "Who needs dates when you're saving the world?"

"I'm sorry, Jacki."

The young woman pushed her thick black glasses up on the bridge of her nose. "Don't be. I think he only asked me out because he wants me to help him pass his chemistry class."

"Loser!" Libby called out from the other side of the room.

"I agree. Drop him before it's too late." Matt peeked out from the open doors of the specimen storage cabinet.

Sassa wanted to smile but she looked for Jacki's reaction before commenting.

The young woman shrugged. "I hate it when they're right."

Sassa nodded. "Yes, but you love it that they care so much."

"Yeah. It's nice."

Yes, it is. How fortunate she was—they were—to have this team, each other's support.

Sassa took a deep breath. "Hey, I just… I… Thank you."

Across the way, Matt smiled. "For Sam…and you."

Jacki nodded. "Yeah. We're family."

Libby set the case of slides on the table and held her

hands out for Keri. "Come on. Give me our precious girl and let's get started."

Tears filled Sassa's eyes and slipped down. She wiped them quickly. "We're going to do it this time. I know it."

Matt lined up the samples.

Sassa carefully measured the viruses. She placed them on the tray and slid it inside the glass case.

"Matt, make sure the propane is hooked up. If this does work, I want to be able to kill it." As he walked away, she added, "Make sure the liquid nitrogen is functional, too."

Libby bounced a fussy Keri as she stood next to Sassa. "Are you that confident?"

Sassa's jaw tightened. "Yes."

Jacki inhaled sharply. Matt turned the propane valve and ignited the burner. Once that was done, he checked the liquid nitrogen regulators. "All set."

Sassa took a deep breath. "All right. Let's do this." She slid her hands into the container's gloves. She didn't need to recheck the formula. She had it memorized now. Flexing her fingers in the awkward gloves, she dropped the first sample onto a glass slide.

"Here we go." She added the second virus to the slide. No one moved. Voices echoed in the hall outside and stopped by their door. Still no one moved. The voices rose in volume. Still no one moved.

"There!" Matt pointed. "It's growing."

He was right. The same structure Sassa had seen on Sam's plate appeared—green tinted, resembling mold, growing exponentially.

"That's it," Sassa murmured. "Growing just as fast as when Sam did it."

"Do you want me to fire up the propane, Sassa?" Matt's voice sounded tense.

"Yes. Now. Do it."

Flame shot into the container, directed at the growth on the glass slide, and burned for a long minute. Matt turned off the valve. They waited silently for the flames to die down. All that was left on the slide was black ash.

No one said a word as reality hit them.

Then Jacki grabbed Sassa's arms. "You did it, Sassa! You did it!"

Sassa closed her eyes for one long moment. When she opened them, Matt pulled her into a hug.

Gripping his waist, she reached for Jacki and smiled at Libby. "*We* did it. I couldn't have done it without you three."

Suddenly the lab door opened. They all jumped, spun and stepped protectively in front of the container. Sassa could almost hear the collective sigh when they realized it was the agent assigned to guard Sassa.

Agent Paulsen paused for a moment before coming all the way in the room. "Sorry for the interruption. Ms. Nilsson, there's a man here who says he's Erik Larsen."

Sassa's heart fell to her toes. "Erik's here?"

"He claims that's his name, ma'am. I'm not letting him anywhere near you until I get clearance. I just wanted you to know."

Sassa shook her head. "Thanks. I appreciate that."

"Just doing my job, ma'am." The agent exited.

Matt turned frowning features toward her. "Do you think it's really him?"

"I don't know. But I'm not dealing with him until we finish here." She shook her head. "Leave it to Erik to show up and ruin a great moment. Let's get this cleaned up."

Sassa took Keri from Libby's arms and placed a kiss on her daughter's head. Then she checked her phone. Almost two hours and still Jared hadn't called her. Now that she knew the formula was correct, the hacker's access to her computer took on epic proportions.

Please, Lord. Please make Jared call me.

She checked her phone twice more while they completed the cleanup and found no response. Sassa was excited to tell Jared the news. He would be so relieved. Something must have gone terribly wrong for him not to call and keep her informed. In the meantime, Keri fell into a fretful sleep. Sassa lay her down in the portable crib and left the office to say good-night to her team.

"Thank you all again. I think tomorrow we might actually be able to take the day off. I'll text you and let you know."

Matt hesitated. "What about the man outside? I'll stick around if you want."

Sassa shook her head. "Go home. If it is Erik, I need to handle him on my own."

Libby gave her a quick hug. "Don't let him bring you down, Sass. You've done an amazing thing here."

Sassa gipped her hand. "We did an amazing thing."

Libby returned her smile and headed to the door. Sassa followed her friends. Agent Paulsen stood outside. "Did you get your clearance, Agent?"

He nodded. "He checks out. He is Erik Larsen. Agent Kopack said it's up to you if you want to see him."

Sighing, Sassa nodded. "Send him in. But stay close. If I call, you can escort him out."

"You got it. Oh, and Agent Kopack wanted me to tell you they got the Spyder."

Relief flooded over Sassa in a wave. "Did they get the formula?"

"Officer De Luca is checking that out now, ma'am. Kopack said they'd let you know as soon as they find out."

Sassa walked back into the lab and slid her hands into the pockets of her lab coat. More good news. Libby was right. She couldn't allow Erik to steal her sense of victory. Now that she had the formula, she was one step away from finding a cure and this nightmare would be over.

The door opened. Her ex stepped into the room. Still handsome. Dirty-blond hair, short, slightly curly on top. His blue eyes stood out against his dark tan, fake of course. Erik was never outside long enough to tan. His cheeks seemed a bit gaunt. In fact, as he walked closer, she could see the strains of hard living. Lines around his mouth and eyes. Dull skin and shots of gray in his hair. He'd aged. Still, his features bore the same carefree smile. She knew all too clearly what was behind that smile. He really didn't care. That was the point.

He came closer, almost as if he was going to embrace her, and she stepped back.

His arms fell down. "Well, I thought you might be a little glad to see me."

She gave a small, bitter laugh. "Those days are long gone, Erik."

The smile faded. "Yeah, I guess that's true."

"I suppose you're here because you heard about Sam."

"Yes, I'm sorry, Sassa. I know how much he meant

to you. The news isn't saying much but I know Sam and his dangerous work. All this hyped-up security tells me I was right."

She closed her eyes. "Stop the nonsense, Erik. We both know you didn't come here out of concern for me. You came to see what you could bleed out of this situation."

He let his head dip. After a few moments of silence, he lifted his gaze and the look in his blue eyes chilled her to the bone. "How can you say that, Sas? I'm here to make sure my baby is safe." He looked toward the office where the top of Keri's crib was barely visible. Erik moved toward it.

Sassa took two quick steps to block his path. "Never. You won't use her for your selfish purposes. I'll never let that happen. I was granted full custody two months ago for reasons of abandonment. You don't have any say in what happens to her."

He shook his head. "How is it going to look in court when I tell them I didn't even know about my baby?"

"You can't win. I have witnesses and proof."

"I don't know. I can be pretty convincing." He raised his hands and his facial expression changed to one of sadness. "Your Honor, I didn't even know I had a daughter. I've been cheated out of time with my precious girl."

Sassa's blood froze. Erik didn't have a leg to stand on legally. But images of days and days in court, months of lawyers' bills and years of constant strain flashed through her mind. She could see it all, as if it had already happened. His whole, horrible plan came to fruition in her imagination. "You had this planned all along, didn't you? You wanted me to get established so you could come back and suck me dry." She shook her head. "It won't work, Erik. I won't pay you to stay away."

"Like I said, I can be very convincing. I was in your way. I wanted my lovely wife to succeed and our constant battles wore her down. So, I left and lost out on time with my child. But everything I've done is for my family." He raised his hands again in that mocking way. "We can't live together but I still love my wife, Your Honor. I'm just not as successful as her. I'll need help supporting our precious girl."

The boy she had once loved had well and truly died. The man who stood before her bore no resemblance to the hopeful, earnest person he had once been. She pointed to the door. "Your threats are not going to work. Get out."

"Oh, I will, but I won't go far. I need to keep an eye on my future."

Another sensation filtered through her. Fear. She hated what Erik had become, but that didn't mean she wanted to see him dead. "Don't be crazy, Erik. You need to stay away from us. You don't know the people who are involved. They killed Sam and June. They're seriously dangerous."

He smirked a smile of pure evil. "Baby, so am I."

SIX

As soon as Kopack told Jared that Erik Larsen had showed up, Jared left the police station. The last thing Sassa needed was that guy sticking his nose into her business, confusing her and stressing her out. He pulled into the university parking lot and took the stairs of the lab building two at a time. The agents nodded as he passed through the doors and Agent Paulsen greeted him in the hall.

"Is Larsen still in there?"

"Yeah, and I don't like it. That guy is trouble."

"You're right about that."

Jared strode to the door and walked in. Sassa stood across the room, between Larsen and the office… between him and Keri. Her features were ashen. The stricken look on her face made Jared see red.

He glared at Larsen. "Get out. Don't come around here again or I'll see to it you end up behind bars."

Erik didn't move until Agent Paulsen stepped in behind Jared. The agent's presence lent support to Jared's authority.

Only then did Erik move toward Jared. His gaze went up and down Jared's taller figure as he passed.

"So you're what's coming between me and my wife."
He looked back at Sassa. "That will look good in court,
too."

Jared didn't understand what Larsen meant, but by
the look on Sassa's face his words terrified her. Larsen
strode past him and out the door. Agent Paulsen followed him and closed the door behind them.

"What was that all about?"

"Something you just made worse."

"How could I have made it worse? That guy screams
trouble without any help from me."

Sassa's whole body bristled. He knew her well
enough to know she felt trapped, and whenever she
felt trapped the snark came out.

"He's just trying to frighten me."

"It seems like he did a good job."

"It's not your problem, Jared."

"Not my problem? What's going on, Sassa? You've
been shutting me out for two days. What happened?"

"Erik is my problem. I don't need you to fight my
battles for me. I need to take care of it on my own."

"We're partners in this, remember? Or at least, we're
supposed to be. Instead, you're wasting energy fighting me."

She took a deep breath and finally met his gaze.
"I'm not fighting you, Jared. I don't fight. I confront
my problems, meet them head-on. I force myself…and
others…to face the truth. That includes you."

Her words rang true and that gave him pause. She
did confront things. Met them head-on with courage
and didn't back down, even if she feared the outcome…
even if it hurt. And Sassa could be easily hurt. Jared
knew that to be true. When she loved, she loved hard

and fought for anyone she cared about. He admired that in her, had even appreciated it once when she showed signs of defending him. She stood across from him now, tired, her hair pulled up in a messy knot at the top with straggles hanging down, gentle reminders of the soft heart beneath her hard exterior.

She met his gaze. "I'm brutally honest with myself. I don't hide from my fears and I expect others to do the same. That's why I confront issues…mine as well as others'."

There was purpose and meaning behind her sentence. He frowned. "What are you trying to say?"

"I'm saying it's time to be honest with each other."

"We're fighting to keep you out of the hands of killers. I don't how much more brutally honest we can get."

"We can't have a relationship, Jared. Nothing can happen between us."

He rolled his eyes and looked away. "This is because of the kiss, isn't it? It was just a simple gesture of relief, Sassa. It meant nothing."

She hesitated then gave him a nod. "I'm glad to hear it. But that makes this a good time to clear the air. I think you've been avoiding the truth."

"I'm avoiding the truth?" Her statement threw him off guard. Wasn't she the one overreacting to a kiss to the top of her head? A kiss that even now brought to mind the orange-blossom scent that surrounded her… but still. It was just a natural reaction…wasn't it?

His own confused mind made him unprepared for her next statement.

"Every time you talk about your divorce, you blame yourself. But it was your wife who walked away. Why is that, Jared?"

The turn of the conversation made him uncomfortable so he redirected it. "You're one to talk. Your past just walked by me and I'm certain he's here to threaten the thing you love most." He glanced at the office where Keri slept.

"You're right. He is here for that but I had enough sense to walk away. I fought him then and I'll fight him again. But every time you talk about the failure of your marriage, you take all the blame when your ex-wife is just as much at fault. That leads me to believe you're still in love with her."

"In love with my wife? Is that what you think?"

He stared at her. He wasn't in love with Jessica. Hadn't been since…well, since he'd met Sassa. That realization brought him up short.

Two short weeks ago he would have not believed the righteous words directed toward him. But they were true and he also recognized that her bristling emotions were *for* him. She couldn't hide her soft, hurting heart, so she covered it up with smart remarks and brutal honesty. Still…all that emotion was for him…for the hurt she thought he still carried over his divorce.

Standing in front of him, bristling with anger, ready to fight for him… Sassa was the most beautiful thing he'd ever seen, one he wanted to kiss…for real this time.

Closing the space between them, he pulled her into his arms.

At first, his actions startled her, but soon her hands gripped his waist and she kissed him back. Her lips were sweet from the citrus-flavored lip balm she always used, and she smelled like a warm summer's night filled with the scent of orange blossoms… Everything he loved wrapped up in this one woman.

It was a kiss he never wanted to end. Their lips felt so right together, as if he'd been waiting all his life for this. Finally, he had to let her go just to breathe. She took two steps back. Her eyes stayed closed and she pressed two fingers to her mouth. That little movement told him she felt the same jolt of recognition he had felt. He almost kissed her again just to make sure it was real, but she took another step back and opened her eyes, those beautiful blue eyes, the color of the Caribbean seas.

"Did you just kiss me to prove that you don't love your wife?"

"Of course not…" Another lie. No more lies between them. It was time for the truth. He shook his head. "Yes, it started that way. But it didn't stay like that. It was a real kiss. Just you and me, with no one and nothing between us."

She swallowed. He watched the movement of her throat, the way her pulse pounded in her neck, and wondered how he'd ever thought she was anything but perfect.

His phone rang. He stifled a frustrated sound, pulled it out of his pocket and silenced it. But it rang again. It was Kopack.

Gritting his teeth, he answered. "Hello?"

"I need you at the hospital. Now. Our little hacker tried to slash her wrists with a piece of metal she pulled from a table in the booking room. We rushed her here and now she's talking up a storm."

"I'll be right there." Jared pocketed his phone and looked at Sassa. "I have to go, but this isn't over."

She shook her head and the soft curls brushed her face in a way that made it hard for Jared to concentrate on her words.

"Yes, it is. It was over before it began. You're trapped in your past, Jared. It has made you what you are. It makes you…aspire. You're constantly reaching for something, an exciting life, a successful career…an accomplished woman."

She paused and pinned him with her piercing blue-eyed gaze. "I'm not that woman."

With that, she turned, walked to the office and shut the door behind her. But as soon as it closed, she jerked it open and marched back.

"When you see Kopack, let him know I just did another test. I got it right and the Spyder has the formula."

Jared plugged the hospital's address into the GPS of his vehicle. He kept screwing it up and had to do it three times before he inputted it correctly and was on his way.

That last impetuous kiss kept invading his thoughts. Sassa's sweet, orange-flavored taste lingered on his lips… He shook his head.

Why did he do it?

It was definitely a stupid move. Now he couldn't stop thinking about it. Not that Sassa was ever far from his thoughts. She was an enigma to him. Every time he thought he had her figured out, she threw something else at him. If he didn't duck his head, it would hit him right in the face. Kind of like the punch the Spyder had thrown at him on the roof.

He needed to be thinking about the Black Knights' young, virulent IT hacker, not Sassa and her soft curves, sweet lips and ever-changing moods.

Did she really think she was not an accomplished woman? She was the most accomplished woman he'd ever met. That was one of the things that kept him constantly intrigued. He never quite knew what would come out of her.

Like when she said he aspired. *Aspire*. The word made him itch. Earlier she'd said he was overly ambitious. It seemed she'd tried to tone that accusation down and changed it to "aspire." It didn't have quite the same negative implications. Still… He shifted in his seat.

It wasn't a bad word. As far as motives went, it was pretty good. Why shouldn't he reach for more? He didn't have much to hang on to in his life.

The light turned red and he braked to a stop.

A memory of his mother's voice drifted through his mind. She had a lovely singing voice. When he was very young, she used to sing to him every night. He'd fall asleep with her hand in his hair and a soft lullaby easing him into his dreams.

But those were the early years, before alcohol became more important to her than her son. He'd stuffed the memory away because it popped up at awkward times and reminded him of what he'd lost.

As a young college student, he remembered sitting on the city bus on his way to visit his dying mother in the hospital. A young boy across from him had leaned his head on his mother's shoulder. Envy had gripped Jared's soul so tightly, he couldn't breathe. He'd turned away and gotten off the bus at the next stop. He'd ended up walking the rest of the way to the hospital, almost a mile away.

Children and a family life had never even been a topic of discussion between him and Jessica. Mainly because he'd put those painful memories far away, into the darkest recesses of his mind…until Sassa had dragged them out again.

Yes, she confronted issues, everyone's issues, his included. But some of those confrontations were just too painful to bring out into the open.

No matter what she said, it wasn't wrong to aspire. He wanted…deserved more and he would keep reaching for it. He didn't fault Sassa for her need to confront. It was her way of coping. But some things were better left buried.

Sassa was right. There could never be anything between them. There was no common ground linking their two attitudes. No meeting place for people with such different approaches…even if she had the softest lips and the sweetest smell of orange blossoms surrounded her. He couldn't let those temptations lead him astray again.

A car honked behind him. The light had turned green. Lost in his thoughts, Jared hadn't noticed. He accelerated quickly, determined to keep his mind on the job at hand.

The Spyder. Jared didn't know why Kopack needed him at the hospital. What could the girl's suicide attempt have to do with him? He pulled into the parking lot and hurried into the building and up the elevator to her room.

Kopack met him outside her closed door. "Just in time. The Spyder's been asking for you."

"Me? Why?"

"I have no clue. But those are the only words coming out of her mouth. We can't get her to tell us anything else. Not even her real name and, so far, her fingerprints haven't turned up. We don't know who she is or where she comes from. Nothing. I'm hoping she'll talk to you."

Jared shrugged. "I'll give it a shot. But don't hold out too much hope. Chekhov's recruits would rather die."

"She got pretty close. She's weak and her health is still in danger. I had to use some harsh words to convince her doctors to let you talk to her."

Jared took a deep breath. "Let's go find out what Miss Spyder wants with me."

Kopack opened the door and they stepped inside. The agent stopped near the door and let Jared move closer. Stretched out on the bed, the deadly Spyder seemed tiny and almost fragile. It made it hard to remember she'd tried to bite his face.

They'd secured both her arms to the bed railing. Gauze wrapped around her wrists and hands, securing them to boards so she could barely move her fingers. Needles punctured the insides of both elbows and tubes ran from them to machines beside the bed. Her black hair fanned out on the pillow, her face almost as pale as the white pillowcase beneath her head.

Her eyes were closed but as he walked toward her, her lids popped open. Silent, she watched him approach. Her dark eyes seemed almost black and flashed with suppressed fury as she scoured his features.

When he stopped at her bedside, her lips parted but she couldn't speak. She had to lick her lips to try again.

"Your pretty face is bruised." Her voice was weak and raspy.

He'd been so involved with Sassa, he hadn't noticed. He touched his cheek where Spyder had hit him and winced.

"I'm glad it hurts," whispered the little Spyder. "I wish I'd broken your nose."

Taken aback, Jared stared at her. He shouldn't be

surprised. The manager at the building where she was captured had attested to her willingness to hurt people—and right now...him.

Why did she harbor what seemed to be a special hate for him? Because he'd captured her?

No. Her feelings seemed to go back further than that. Were her strong emotions for him a weakness he needed to probe? If so...how far should he go? Kopack had said her health was still unstable. One misstep on his part could unbalance that precarious position.

Sassa's safety depended on the information in this young woman's head. Jared would go as far as he needed.

Stepping forward, he touched her fingers taped to the board. He expected her to flinch—a response he would have understood if she hated people. Instead, two of her fingers slid over his and clasped them against the board. The desperate, almost needy, gesture sent shivers of revulsion up his spine.

Jared swallowed, wondering what to do next. At a loss, he finally said, "Why would you want to break my nose? You don't even know me."

Her dark almost-black eyes fired up. "I've read everything I could find about you, and my little webs go everywhere. I know all about you, everything there is to know. You pretty boys are all the same. Beautiful bodies. Strong arms. Wonderful mouths...mouths that spout poisonous lies."

She stroked his fingers then pressed on them painfully. Jared itched to jerk his hand away but she was getting emotional. Maybe she'd let something slip if he pushed harder.

"I don't tell lies."

"Yes, you do. You all do! You probably have pretty little Sassa wrapped around your finger."

Jared must have showed his surprise because she smiled. "Yes, I know all about her, too. I've been watching both of you. I know your pasts, your financials. I even watch you on the campus cameras. I'm the one that gave Heiser the idea to snatch the baby." She jerked, raising her head up off the pillow.

"I know you and you're just like all the others." She pressed so hard on his fingers it forced him to pull away.

"Everything you say is a lie. You think you're all so smart...all you clever Cambridge boys with your soft touches and sweet promises. But I'm smarter. I outwit you every time. I take away your Kensington homes, your Lamborghinis and the models you love. Even the smart ones, like your Sassa. You think she's smart enough to outwit me? I switched her precious little formula just to throw her off."

"You changed the formula on the computer just to mess with Sassa's head?"

She strained against the bonds on her arms. "I won't just mess with her head. As soon as I get out of here, I'll find a keyboard and I'll get her."

"The only thing you'll get is a jail sentence."

Her laugh was almost a crazy shriek. "You think jail will hold me? I broke your team's pathetic security system. Mark thinks he's so clever but I broke his program!"

So Mark was right. She knew his name. How could she have such a comprehensive understanding of their IT departments? He stepped back, stunned by the depth of her knowledge.

"See... I told you I'm smarter than all of you. My

spider webs are everywhere. I have servers right under your noses, linked to your own. You'll never find me."

Her crazy laugh pierced the room again. "I'll break any jail's system and be out before you know it. Just watch. I'll—"

Her tirade broke off and she fell back upon her pillow, unconscious. She'd been so worked up and straining so hard, the machine beside her bed gave off an alarm. Another alarm on the other side began to beep. A nurse hurried into the room to her bedside.

Jared stepped closer to the bed. "Is she all right?"

"Her blood pressure is too high. You have to leave."

Jared nodded and stepped out. Kopack followed close behind. The Spyder's virulent madness seemed to follow Jared outside the room. He ran a hand across the back of his neck, trying to shake off her lingering presence.

"Well, that was just about the sickest love-hate scene I've ever witnessed." Kopack was shaken, too.

Jared shrugged his shoulders. "Yeah, it's going to take me a while to get over it."

Kopack grasped his shoulder and gave it a shake. "You did good, De Luca. She gave us a lot of information. We'll be checking the Cambridge records. Obviously, she has some connection with the university and there can't be too many Lamborghini owners who lived in Kensington, dated models and lost it all. We'll connect the dots and she'll be going to jail for the rest of her life."

"Yeah, it's a lot of information, but it will take a long time to sort it all out, time we don't have. Sassa ran another test and succeeded. She recreated the formula and it's on her computer. If Spyder sent the information to

Chekhov, he'll move quickly to develop it. We're running out of time."

Kopack tightened his grip on Jared's shoulder. "Don't jump the gun. We don't know that she sent the formula on to Chekhov. It sounded to me like she was too busy playing games with you and Sassa to do her job. Our IT guys are working on her computers. They'll let us know what she did. In the meantime, let's celebrate our successes. We haven't had too many. You scored big points for us in there."

"I'm not sure I had much to do with it. All I had to do was show up."

"Must have been that pretty face. It does things to women."

Jared chuckled. "Yeah…right. My pretty face isn't getting me any points with Sassa."

Kopack paused. "Are you trying to score points with her?"

Jared kicked himself for his slip of the tongue. "No, of course not. I'm just trying to work with her prickly personality."

The agent studied his features for a long while. Then he nodded. "Good. Keep your distance. You have a talent for fieldwork. There aren't many people who can step in and perform as well as you have. You stay calm and think quickly. There's always a place for those skills."

Talent. Skills.

The words reverberated through Jared. Stunned, he watched Kopack walk away. After a few feet, the agent paused and turned back. "Come on. Let's get your info to the computer guys at the office. They need to get their searches started."

Jared stumbled into action and followed.

* * *

After Jared left the lab, Keri woke and wouldn't let Sassa put her down even for a moment. Her first tooth was making her fussy…and maybe she was all too aware of her mother's tension.

Poor baby. Her world had turned topsy-turvy. These weeks had been hard for her. First her mother had gone for a whole week on the trip to China. Then Grandma had left and a strange man had invaded her world. Although, if Sassa was honest, that was one change Keri seemed happy about. She loved Jared. And if Sassa was even more honest, so did she. The kiss proved that.

A kiss that felt so right. No man's touch had ever made her feel safe, protected and respected at the same time. Jared had always treated her as an intelligent human being. So often men looked at her long blond hair, blue eyes, petite size and treated her like a baby doll. She hated that. Jared had never treated her like that…ever.

And he made her laugh. How long had it been since she'd laughed, really laughed? Not a little lift of the lips that acknowledged a clever word or joke. No, Jared made her laugh, sometimes even against her will. He almost dragged it out of her, forcing her to enjoy life.

She smiled, thinking of Jared, and clutched Keri close to her. She loved how he loved her child. But most of all, she loved how he made her feel that together they could do anything.

Truth be told, she simply loved Jared.

Sassa took a deep breath. It wasn't fair. But it was the truth. She loved Jared but he would leave. He had goals and plans that Sassa and Keri didn't fit into.

When he went, he would take a piece of her heart.

But she would let him go…and she would be thankful that he had protected her and her daughter, thankful he had awakened her will to live and, most of all, the desire to love again.

She would try to remember that in the days ahead… and would try to be thankful rather than dwell on what might have been because she was certain Jared was going places. Kopack had come to depend on him. Jared had started out the investigation as someone on the fringes but had managed to make himself an integral part. All the opportunities Jared had always dreamed about would be waiting for him on the other side of this nightmare.

What would be waiting for her?

Court troubles with Erik. And how would she fight him with no money? She doubted she'd have a job here at the university. Dean Trujillo, head of the department, did not like her. The only reason she'd had a job was that Sam had fought for her and made it happen. Now that he was gone…

Still, she had proved herself. She'd discovered the formula for the pathogen. Surely some university would appreciate her skills. Maybe not here but somewhere…

She shook her head. It had been eventful day. She just needed a break. She hurried to the lab door and opened it. Agent Paulsen greeted her.

"Do you think we could go home for the night?" She hadn't been to her house in days. Keri needed a bath and a good night's rest in her crib. Sassa wanted a real shower in the comfort of her own home, not one of the lab's facilities.

"I don't see why not. Let me run it through Kopack." Sassa turned back inside and gathered Keri's diaper bag and their dirty clothes. When the agent signaled the okay, she was ready.

Once outside her house, she sat in the car as the agents searched and secured it. When at long last she stepped inside, home didn't seem like home. That closed-up scent drifted over her again, the same one she'd sensed when she'd first returned from China. Had it only been three weeks ago? If felt like ages.

Agent Paulsen handed her the keys. Standing at her door, they both turned as another vehicle pulled up and parked across the street. Paulsen turned back. "It's your ex-husband. He's been hanging around."

Erik? Hanging around? Her feeling of dread must have showed in her features because the agent said, "Don't worry. We'll make sure he doesn't bother you again."

Sassa gave him a rueful grin. "Can you stay for the rest of my life?"

The agent smiled. "We'll be right outside. Two agents in the back and two in front. Get some rest. You could use it."

His kinds words brought tears to her eyes. Sensing her mother's despair, Keri began to fuss. "It's all right, baby. Mommy's all right." Stifling her tears, Sassa smiled at the agent. "Thank you."

She lifted Keri higher and closed the door. "Come on. Let's get you something to eat."

She hurried to the kitchen and pulled Keri's favorite fruit out of the freezer. With her tooth giving her trouble, Keri's appetite had dropped. So try as she might, Sassa could only get a few bites of her daughter's favorite peaches down her. Finally, she gave up. "Let's get a bath and a bottle. You need sleep as much as Mommy."

The bath seemed to relax Keri. She played in her pen long enough for Sassa to shower. With her hair wet, she heated a bottle for Keri and curled up on the couch. Finally, they both began to relax and drifted off.

Something jolted Sassa awake. She looked around. The lamps were still on. Light filled every dark corner. Keri slept peacefully in her arms. So what had disturbed her? Had she heard a noise or was she dreaming?

Clutching Keri to her chest, she sat up and looked around. Should she call Agent Paulsen? Before she could decide, there were scuffling sounds and murmured grunts at the front door. It sounded like someone fell against it.

Pop! The sound came from the outside, at the front corner of the house. Sassa crouched low on the couch cradling Keri beneath her body.

Was that a gunshot?

Someone shouted. "Who are you? What are you doing here?"

Sassa's blood froze. Erik. Why was he out of his car?

Another gunshot. A cry… Erik's voice again.

Sassa's heart pounded like mad. Should she open the door? Did she dare peek out the window or should she just stay in place until Agent Paulsen gave her the all-clear signal? She couldn't move from her position low on the couch, her gaze jumping from the front door down the length of the dark kitchen to the back door.

Suddenly, glass shattered. The back door slammed open and banged against the wall. A black pant leg stepped over the shattered glass and into her kitchen.

Mikhail Chekhov pushed past the broken shards of the doorjamb, jerked his black leather jacket back into place and marched toward her in the exact same manner as he had marched toward Sam in the airport.

For one excruciating moment, Sassa didn't know what to do. What could she do? How could she stop him with her daughter in her arms?

She must have clutched Keri too tightly because she began to cry. Her daughter's fright galvanized Sassa into action. With strength she didn't know she possessed, she leaped to her feet and shifted Keri to one arm. From the nearby end table, she jerked up the Tiffany-style lamp, pulled the cord clean out of the socket and threw it at Chekhov's head with enough force to spin it in the air.

He raised his arm to protect his face, hitting at the stained-glass sections of the lamp. Pieces broke free and colored fragments flew toward his face, slicing into his cheek. But he only paused for a moment… just long enough for Sassa to run to the door, unbolt it and throw it open. She almost tripped over the body of Agent Paulsen. Halting just in time, she hopped over him and lunged down the stairs. Another body lay on the ground to her left. She heard scuffling from around the corner but she never stopped or looked back.

Way down the street, blue lights flashed. Sirens echoed over the night air. Sassa ran out into the street toward the oncoming cars. Headlights flashed over her and she halted, clutching her now screaming baby to her breast.

A tall, familiar form, shadowed behind the lights, stepped out of a vehicle and ran to her. Other agents poured from the cars and ran toward the house.

Sassa sobbed with relief and fell into Jared's arms.

"Are you all right?"

She tried to answer but she was crying too hard. She

buried her face against his chest. The familiar scent of pine drifted over her. She was safe. Truly safe. Relief swept over her, but shock was taking hold. She couldn't stop crying.

Finding no comfort from her mother, Keri reached for Jared. He hefted her into one arm but kept the other wrapped securely around Sassa.

Even her daughter felt safe with him. That thought made her cry even more.

"I'm sorry. So, so sorry. I promise I won't leave your side again until this is over."

They were the sweetest words she'd ever heard. If only she could stop sobbing long enough to tell him so. But she couldn't. All she could do was cling to him as days and days of fear finally broke through her wall of armor. She clung to Jared and tried to calm down. But one thought ran through her mind.

When it is over, how will I survive without him?

Jared surveyed the scene around Sassa's house. Neighbors of the quiet little cul-de-sac gathered on the sidewalk behind the yellow caution tape. Sassa and Keri sat in the back of his SUV. It had taken Jared a long time to calm them both down.

Something had broken inside Sassa. He could sense it. Some sort of dam had been holding back hidden emotions, deep, old feelings. Now that the dam had been breached, she was struggling to get her head above the water. Jared was determined to see that she didn't have to struggle too much more.

He strode over to Kopack, who stood in the middle of Sassa's yard.

"How bad is it?"

"Not good. Chekhov used the same tactic. Some of his younger acolytes distracted the agents in the front. Then he attacked from the back. We found two sets of footprints back there. My agents took down the two young terrorists in front. One of them is barely hanging on. But Chekhov had someone else with him. Another larger man, about a size-eleven shoe, larger than Chekhov's."

Jared shook his head. "We even know Chekhov's shoe size but still we can't catch him."

Kopack made a rude sound. "One of my agents has a concussion. The other has a serious stab wound to the stomach."

"Well, we know which one came in contact with Chekhov. He's lethal with those knives. What do we know about the other man with Chekhov?"

"Now that Heiser is dead, we suspect it was his third in command. A man named Rashad Korgay. He's a Chechnyan dissident with ties to the Russian mafia and black-market weapons dealers." Kopack paused. "Chekhov used a police-grade battering ram to knock down Sassa's door. Korgay has to be the one supplying them with top-of-the-line weapons. The other two Black Knights, the ones my agents took down, are young and still unidentified."

"Chekhov's like a pied piper. How many of these young men and women will he allow to die before we stop him?"

"I don't know but he's hemorrhaging people." The agent looked around. "So am I."

Jared felt Kopack's frustration all the way to the bottom of his toes. "I've asked for help, border agents from our drug section. Those guys have been around the block. They'll give us more manpower and some great insight. They should be here by tomorrow morning."

"Good. We can use the help. By the way, the agent Chekhov stabbed was awake when we arrived. He saw Chekhov leave and he was bleeding badly on his arm. Seems your girl did some damage."

"Sassa will be glad to hear that. She said she threw a Tiffany lamp at him and it shattered."

"Too bad she missed his head."

"She tried." They exchanged grim smiles as EMTs rushed a gurney past them, headed to an ambulance.

Jared inhaled. "Was that Agent Paulsen?"

Kopack nodded. "He was by the front door when two Black Knights attacked. His partner was around the corner doing a search. Paulsen took the brunt of the attack."

"How is he?"

"Not good. He took a shot to the chest. Then both terrorists turned on the other agent. That's when Larsen walked up and intervened. His efforts cost him." Kopack gestured to another body the EMTs were zipping into a body bag. "He lost his life but saved my agent. If Larsen hadn't shouted at them, my agent would probably be dead, too."

"Sassa said she heard her ex's voice. Are you sure it's Larsen?"

"The ID in his wallet identified him."

Jared shook his head. "So he saved one of your agents and died a hero."

"You and I both know that wasn't his reason for showing up here."

Jared grimaced. "No, he heard all about Sassa's sudden popularity."

"He won't need hers. He'll have his own."

Both men were silent as the irony of his last act filtered through their thoughts. Jared wondered how the news would affect Sassa.

"The last terrorist we captured…" Kopack said after a few moments. "He's just a kid. I'm hoping we can crack him and he'll give us more info on the group."

"I wouldn't count on it. All the members attempted to end their lives rather than talk."

Kopack shrugged. "At least maybe we can get numbers out of him. I'd like to know how many Black Knights are left." He shook his head. "We know one thing. The Spyder didn't send her information on to Chekhov."

"How can you be so sure? The IT guys are still checking her computer."

Kopack eyed him. "Do you think Chekhov would have wasted men in such a flagrant attempt to snatch Sassa if he had any idea the formula was available to him by some other means?" Kopack shook his head. "He's still searching and he's getting more desperate… like time is running out for him."

"What do you mean? We've known from the beginning this has been a do-or-die situation for everyone in his organization."

"Maybe they're so desperate because they know their leader doesn't have much time left."

"You think Chekhov's disease is catching up with him?"

"My agent who saw his escape said he was bleeding badly and was pale—so pale, he looked half dead. He looked much worse than our most recent photos show."

"Even if that's true," Jared noted, "Chekhov's death

won't stop the group. They'll keep going until all of them are captured or dead themselves."

The truth of that sat on the cold night air. They both stared at Sassa's little cottage, lights blazing into the dark. Figures moved in and out, gathering evidence and clearing bodies.

Bodies. Jared shook his head. It didn't seem real— like it was a scene from a movie, not his life. All he wanted to do was to snatch Sassa and Keri into his arms and drive away.

He shook his head. "We have to get her away. Some place safe where she can work on the cure."

Kopack paused. "I still can't believe she cracked the code."

"I told you she was brilliant."

"Yes, you did." Kopack studied him with a speculative look that made Jared uncomfortable. "I agree about taking her away. We need to find a safe place. The campus is too busy. Too many bystanders could get hurt. Her house is compromised and, besides, there's not enough room for equipment."

"What kind of equipment?"

"Cameras. Motion detectors. Wires. We need it all. What about her parents' place? You said they had a farm outside of town."

"Near Kingsburg. It's big and somewhat isolated. But hold on… I meant take her someplace secure and far away, like our Washington offices. Taking her to her parents' feels like you're painting a target on her back."

"She already has a target on her back. We're just going to make sure she has lots of barriers between her and the shooters."

Jared shook his head. "I don't like this. You're using Sassa as bait."

Kopack sent him that speculative look again, the one that made him nervous. "You're not thinking, De Luca. We've been here two weeks. We've run through almost every hotel, dive, dump and parking garage in this town. We've had our video guys watching film of every major road and freeway. We've identified cars and narrowed down locations where the Black Knights could be hiding. We're closing the net. If we put Sassa in hiding, they'll go underground, bide their time while they try to locate her. We'll have to start over when they resurface. Not to mention the fact that will give them time to recuperate and maybe even reinforce. How safe do you think she'll be if that happens?"

Jared inhaled slowly. He hated to admit it but Kopack was right. All Sassa needed was a few more weeks, maybe even days, to find the cure. Then the Black Knights would have no more use for her and she would be safe. The best thing they could do was buy her the time she needed.

Kopack must have taken Jared's silence for agreement. He nodded once then said, "As soon as my people have cleared her place of evidence, take her inside and have her pack all the clothes and supplies she needs. She won't be leaving her parents' place until she has the cure…or we have the Black Knights. Whatever comes first." He turned and walked away. After a few steps, he halted, spun and strode back to Jared.

Kopack leaned in close. "You know, De Luca, I've told you before, but it bears repeating. For an officer with no field experience, you've handled yourself exceptionally well. But I'm going to give you one word of caution. Don't become too emotionally involved with your subject. It could cloud your judgment. Those kinds of mistakes will get you both killed."

The agent walked away, leaving Jared shaking his head.

Too late. He'd been emotionally involved with Sassa from the first time he'd met her. Right from the start, she'd intrigued him. Bedraggled, beaten and partially in shock, she'd refused to let Kopack break her. She'd fought back. No. Not fought. Confronted.

It was hard not to be emotionally impacted by a woman who challenged every idea he had, even his feelings for his ex-wife. Sassa had shattered his illusions about Jessica and if he stuck around much longer, she might destroy the rest of his dreams and aspirations. Gritting his teeth, he stuffed down his resentment and headed for his vehicle to tell Sassa her ex-husband was dead.

SEVEN

Jared walked toward the SUV, its blue lights flashing over his face and grim features. Sassa had watched the gurneys go by with bodies encased in bags. Even before he slid inside, she knew what he was going to say.

He opened the back door and slid in.

"One of those bodies was Erik's, wasn't it? He's dead."

Jared shut the door before he spoke. "Yes. Apparently, he saw the altercations and left his car to confront the intruders. The Black Knights turned on him and that enabled the agent to break free."

She stared at him. "His interference saved the agent?"

Jared nodded.

Sassa closed her eyes. A thousand thoughts ran through her mind. The way she'd start a conversation and Erik would take over, determined to be the center of attention in all their interactions, even ones concerning her work, which he knew nothing about. The times he'd come home late at night, after she'd gone to bed, and binge eat because he'd been gambling all day and night. He'd clean out their bank account, then their food, leaving her to scramble for something to eat the next day.

At family gatherings he'd always had some story or joke to share. He'd made everyone laugh and was the life of the party. In their early years, her friends had thought he was wonderful and her concerns had fallen on deaf ears. She was simply the bitter, unhappy girl who lost her scholarship. No one had understood how Erik's need to be great affected everyone who cared about him. And now...

Please, Lord, cleanse my heart of this bitterness. Let me see only good. Let me speak only what You would have me say.

A feeling of peace nipped at the edges of her senses. That sense of peace was strong enough to allow her to say, "I'm glad some good came from his death."

Sassa swallowed as sadness overwhelmed her. "In the end, he got what he always wanted. I'm happy for that, too." Her voice was raspy. Hot tears filled her eyes and slid down her cheeks. "He was a hero for someone."

Keri had finally fallen into a fitful sleep in her arms. Sassa dashed away the tears with one hand. But more followed. Jared wrapped an arm around her and pulled her close. She leaned into his broad shoulder to cry and mourn, not for the man Erik had become, but the one she knew he could have been if only he'd learned to draw on the Lord's strength. How different his life— their life together—would have been.

And yet...here she was again. Falling for another man who didn't know the Lord, who didn't know how to draw on the strength she had just called upon.

She couldn't do it again. She wouldn't.

Wiping her tears, she pushed away from Jared's shoulder. Her tears had soaked his shirt. She touched the wet spot.

"I'm sorry." It felt like she was apologizing for more than just wetting his shirt. Those words went deeper for her.

"Don't be. I'm happy to lend my shoulder to a woman who can forgive like you just did."

His voice, filled with tenderness, shook her to her core. Oh, how she wanted to lean in, to press her face into the curve of his neck, to smell his clean, pine scent and to feel safe. But there was no safety there. The only true safety was in the arms of the Lord.

She wiped her cheeks again. "I haven't forgiven him. He threatened to use Keri against me. It will be a long time before I forgive that. But the Lord gave me the weapon to fight the bitterness by showing me the good that came from Erik's sacrifice."

Jared made a rude noise. "I doubt Erik walked up to those men planning to make the ultimate sacrifice."

Sassa nodded. "No, I'm sure he didn't. But the Lord always finds the good and shows it to His people. A man is alive because of Erik's actions. The Lord finds the good. I'll draw comfort from that."

Jared's arm fell away and he leaned back. "We're back to that again. I'm sorry, Sassa, but I can't see any good in the life I led with my mother."

There it was. The admission she'd been dreading to hear. The hurt she couldn't heal. Once he spoke it out loud, there'd be no turning back, no more pretending. She almost reached out to stop him from speaking. But the look on his face, the hard edges in his features, said it more clearly than words.

"I looked for the good, Sassa. Believe me. I prayed for answers and help every day, and still, every minute with my mother was a struggle to find food. To clean her up after she passed out. To go to school afraid of how I smelled because they had shut the water off and I couldn't shower. Where was God in all that?"

Fresh tears fell, this time for the little boy whose struggle was so horrific. "I don't know why you had to go through that, Jared. But I do know God showed you the way to climb out. Even when you didn't recognize Him, He was working in your life. He gave you your grandfather and that policeman. Didn't you ever wonder why that simple interaction made such an impact on you? I'm certain the Lord made sure you would see the man He meant you to be."

He looked away, the flashing lights reflected across his face. His jaw tightened.

Just a minute movement, but it made Sassa's heart sink. It showed her the truth she'd been avoiding, hoping it wasn't true. But now she had to face it.

Jared couldn't—no, refused—to see how God was working in his life. Sassa hadn't been able to share God's love with Erik. No matter how hard she prayed or talked, her ex-husband had turned away. Why did she dare to think she could succeed with Jared? More important, why was it her fate to fall for men who didn't know God?

Maybe the fault wasn't in the men she loved but in her own faith.

She didn't know the answers. She only knew she couldn't go through it again. As wonderful as Jared was, she couldn't place her hopes and dreams of wholeness with a man who didn't know the Lord. Not again. She just couldn't.

Straightening away from Jared, she created a space

between them and sniffled. "Can you find me some tissues and a phone? I need to call Erik's sister."

Jared heaved a sigh. "Why don't you leave that to Kopack?"

She shook her head. "Sandra has been my friend, stood by me all these years. I have to give her some warning."

In the shadowy light, his jaw tightened even more. "You just can't let anything slide, can you? You have to confront everything." He slid across the seat and climbed out of the vehicle. "I'll see what I can do." Frustration filled his tone.

It seemed like only minutes before he returned carrying a box of tissues and a blanket from the back of her sofa. Leaning in, he set the tissues beside her and spread the blanket over her and Keri. Then he pulled her phone out of his pocket.

"This was on the counter. You might as well use it. I don't think we need to worry about the Black Knights tracing your calls right now."

With that, he shut the door and strode back to the house, his movements as strained and stilted as she felt.

Jared sipped his coffee and looked out the oversize picture window of the Nilsson home. Keri sat on a blanket on the floor, quietly playing with a basket of toys her grandma kept at the house. He didn't know how much longer she'd last quietly playing beside him. She was getting fussy.

They'd arrived long after midnight. Keri's tooth was still bothering her and she'd slept very little. Throughout the night, Jared had heard her fitful cries in the other room. When Sassa stumbled into the kitchen, bleary-eyed and barely coherent, Jared had taken the baby from her arms and sent her back to bed.

Jared's cell phone vibrated with a text message from Mark. The FBI had completed a raid on a remote farmhouse in North Dakota where the Spyder had hidden her server. Mark hadn't finished an exhaustive search of her emails but from his quick examination, it appeared she had not sent a communication to Chekhov. She hadn't known the last formula—from the many ones she'd stolen—was the right one. Sassa had detected her presence in time and never given any indication that she'd succeeded.

Jared sighed. At least that was one worry Sassa could let go. He'd tell her when she woke. She'd only been in bed for an hour but Keri was antsy. She looked like she'd had enough playtime. She rubbed both eyes with tiny fists and a great, gaping yawn almost toppled her to her side.

She was so precious. So unique. And she fit so perfectly here, in this rambling ranch-style house. It suited her…and her mother. The big window in front of him opened onto the view of a large grassy area that rolled down to the river. Winter had taken a toll, turning some grassy areas brown, but fresh new tufts of green were breaking out. Fog drifted across the scene and blocked his view of the river. But Sassa had told him they had their own dock with a boat her father had just put in the river in anticipation of warmer days ahead. Then the cool March weather had rolled back in, along with the tule fog that blanketed nearly all of the Central Valley.

Life slowed to a stop in the fog. He wished it would last, this calm, almost netherworld feeling that came with the thick gray mists. But the weather would not

stop the Black Knights. This lull was just the calm before the storm. He knew it, could feel it in his bones.
It made him restless, anxious, and spoiled what would
have been a perfect time for him.

The Nilsson home was everything he'd ever dreamed
a home could be. A large kitchen area with an island
in the middle. River rock surrounded a large fireplace.
A big-screen TV stood to the left in the corner next to
the oversize picture window that opened onto a grass
lawn that rolled to the river's edge. Comfy beige-leather
couches and chairs framed a large half circle around
the fireplace, the television and the perfect view down
to the water.

Family pictures covered the opposite wall. It was
easy to pick Sassa out in her high school cheerleading
uniform. Even then she'd been slightly curvy but still
held the lean lines of youth. Her face and those blue
eyes were wide open, bright, expectant…like she was
ready to tackle the world.

What changes were just around the corner for her?

He could see Keri in her youthful features. The baby
would grow up to be just as beautiful as her mother. If
he had his way, it would be without the sharp edges.
He took a deep breath.

No, that wasn't true. Last night he'd seen the other
side of Sassa's confrontational attitude. She really did
meet issues head-on and her courage turned bitterness
into a healing balm. She was able to cast off her resentment for Erik and move toward healing almost immediately.

Her abrupt change had shocked him…and filled him
with admiration. He wished he had that gift, the ability

to turn tragedy into triumph. She would say that gift came from God. Maybe it did, but he'd never received it.

He smiled to himself. It was Sassa's way of reaching for more, hoping for something better…aspiring. Maybe they weren't as far apart as he thought. But he wouldn't try to tell her that. She'd only argue.

He still wished he could protect Keri from all that her mother had experienced. Who would have thought one tiny little baby could so perfectly capture his heart? All that really mattered was protecting those two and the life they represented. The Black Knights threatened everything… Sassa and Keri, their heritage and land… life as they all knew it. He couldn't bear the thought of the destruction that would come if they succeeded. The idea hit him like a physical blow. He closed his eyes, wishing he could pray. Wishing he could gather the peace that Sassa talked about. But nothing happened.

Sassa walked out of the bedroom and he opened his eyes. Her beautiful blond hair was down around her shoulders. It curled more so than usual in the damp, morning air. She looked sleepy, warm, and so very kissable. But more than one wall stood between them.

God might answer Sassa's prayers, but not the ones of lost little boys. Not his.

Purposely, he turned back to the window and sipped his coffee.

She came to stand beside him to look out on the gloomy morning. "A foggy day." She inhaled deeply. "I'm glad. It makes me feel insulated from the world, like the Black Knights can't get to us."

Jared's eyebrows rose in surprise. He tried to mask his reaction by keeping his gaze locked on the scene outside. The Black Knights were out there plotting. He knew it. Could feel it.

But if Sassa wanted—needed—a little break from reality, he would not burst that bubble. Besides, he had one piece of good information for her.

"I just got a text from Mark. The FBI has Spyder's server in their possession. It looks like she didn't know you discovered the formula." He smiled. "You did a good job throwing her off with your fake 'failure' report. Not to mention the fact that you kept her busy long enough for us to capture her. She won't be able to hurt anyone ever again."

She studied the scene in front of them. "I'm not sure if that's good news or bad. I almost wish she had told Chekhov she had it. Then he wouldn't be after me."

"True, but we don't have the cure yet. You would still be the world's best hope for solving that problem. Chekhov knows that. I think you'd still be on his radar."

Sassa heaved a heavy sigh. "I wish Kopack would let the university people deliver my equipment so I could get started on the cure."

Jared shook his head. "We don't have time to vet all those delivery people. Chekhov could easily slip one of his younger acolytes into that group. We have more agents arriving this morning. As soon as Kopack's people brief them, they can start the move. Besides, you need to rest today. You're exhausted."

She closed her eyes and took a deep breath. "What I need is that coffee. It smells great." Keri picked that moment to fuss and raise her arms to her mother.

Sassa lifted her daughter and snuggled her face in her neck. "She feels warm. I think she might have a slight temperature."

"She's been fussy. I think you woke up just in time. She's done with playtime."

Sassa hitched Keri onto her hip and turned to face him. "Thank you. I think I needed that sleep. And thank you…"

Her words dropped off. She licked her lips but didn't turn her gaze away. "Thank you for everything. For watching over us. For taking such good care of Keri."

He nodded but had to turn away. The deep sincerity in her voice was doing things to his insides. Things he didn't need awakened. "You're welcome. But it wasn't hard. She's a constant reminder of everything we're trying to protect."

He gestured to the yard and the gazebo near the water. "I never had this kind of home, but this is what I always dreamed it was like."

She was silent for a long moment before she said, "Yes, I had it all and blew it."

He studied her and she met his gaze unflinchingly. "Jared, I said some things stood between us."

"Some? You said a lot of things stood between us."

"Okay. There're many things between us. I just want you to know that not all of them are your issues. I have my own issues. I had everything going for me, great parents, a wonderful brother…the whole town thought the world of me and I let them down. I had so many benefits and so much potential, and I wasted it all try-ing to change Erik."

He gave her a rueful grin. "Seems to me Jesus had something to say about that. Isn't there a parable about the shepherd leaving the flock to go after the one lamb?"

She shook her head. "For someone who claims he doesn't believe, you sure know a lot of parables."

He turned his gaze back to the yard. "I didn't say I don't believe." He motioned to the view with his coffee mug. "I look at this and I know there is a God. I just don't think He pays much attention to my problems."

"He always pays attention, Jared. We're the ones who don't listen. If I'd stuck to what I knew was right, things would have been different."

Frustration filled him and he met her gaze. "You've paid for your mistakes over and over again. You even lost your first baby. Don't you think that was punishment enough? Do you have to keep paying forever?"

She ducked her head. "I said I have issues of my own. And yes, one of them might be punishing myself for my mistakes. But I do know they have made me who I am today."

There it was again, that ability to turn tragedy into triumph. It was one of the things he found most appealing about her. A golden curl had fallen forward to tickle her cheek. He tucked it behind her ear. A soft blond curl twisted around his finger and he twirled it a little tighter.

Never taking his eyes off the curl wrapped around his finger, he said, "I only see a strong, vital woman who learned how to move on. Maybe you disappointed a lot of people, but you didn't let it stop you. And now you have one of God's wonders in your arms. You have no reason to look back. You can only look forward, especially now. She needs you more than ever."

Sassa's lips parted in surprise. Those beautiful blue eyes told him how much she appreciated his words.

She reached for his hand and pulled it to her lips. Jared caught his breath.

His phone rang.

They both jumped in surprise. Sassa ducked her head and stepped back.

Jared gritted his teeth and pulled the phone out of his pocket. It was Lucero, the lead agent on their guard detail.

"Didn't want to call earlier. I thought you folks might still be asleep, but now I see you're awake, we'd better start our radio check-ins."

"How did you know we were awake?"

"Turn around."

Jared had been facing the living room. Now he turned and looked out the large window toward the water's edge. The fog had momentarily cleared and the agent stood at the end of the boat dock. He waved. Jared signaled back.

"You've got the radio, right?"

"Yes, I'll turn it on." Jared hurried to the kitchen counter where he'd set the radio last night when they arrived and turned it on.

Agent Lucero's voice came over it loud and clear. "I'll radio every hour to check in."

"Got it. Thanks." Jared clicked off. Worst timing possible…or maybe the best. He didn't know anymore. Sassa confused him too much. No matter what the answer, the moment had been lost.

Sassa headed to the kitchen. "I'm starving, how about you?"

"Yep. Sure am. But I checked the fridge and it's clean as a whistle."

She smiled. "My mother planned to be gone for a whole month. Of course it's cleaned out. Probably the cupboards, too. But I know where she keeps her secret stash."

She handed Keri to him. She fussed a little but Jared bounced her. "Hey, hey? What's this? Are you whining at me?"

He lifted her up. She leaned into his arms and Jared gave her a cuddle. "You'd better hurry. I think little miss here is ready for a nap."

"I'd like to get some food down her first…if I can."

Jared heard the door leading to the garage open and shut before Sassa returned with a bag of frozen waffles, a jar of home-canned peaches for Keri and another jar of homemade jelly.

"Is that what I think it is?"

"Yes, my mother's fair-award-winning peach jelly." She held the jar up triumphantly. "With this and frozen waffles, we will feast!"

Jared laughed. "I haven't had homemade jelly since…"

He paused. Not since his grandfather had passed. He smiled, thinking of the older man and how he would have loved Sassa's home and her family.

She pulled a toaster out of the cupboard. "If you'll pop these in the toaster, I'll try to get Keri to eat. I'd feel better if she had something in her tummy."

"Sure. I can a do a mean toaster."

Sassa laughed as she took Keri from his arms. He wasn't sure if he'd ever heard her laugh, really laugh. It was a nice sound. One he could easily get accustomed to. If only…

He put that thought of his mind and concentrated on the frozen waffles.

It didn't take long before they were sitting at the kitchen nook with paper plates in front of them. Keri sat in her high chair and turned her head every time Sassa tried to spoon a dollop of cold peaches into her mouth.

"I give up. If she won't eat her favorite, she won't eat anything."

Jared licked a drip of peach jelly from his finger. "If you don't grab a waffle now, I'll finish all this for you."

"It is good, isn't it? It's my mother's secret recipe. She won't share it with anyone…except me, of course… if I can ever find the time to be in the kitchen so she can teach me how to cook."

"Invite her down to the lab. You can cook up a pretty mean pathogen."

She burst out laughing and covered her full mouth with her hand. Jared grinned. He liked making her laugh, making her happy.

"Do you have a peach orchard on your property?"

"Just a few trees in the back. Most of our crops are lemons and grapes."

"You said your roots go way back. Your family helped settle this area?"

She nodded and dipped her head as a dab of jelly spilled over. She licked it off her lip. "My great-grandfather and grandmother bought the land in the 1800s and started with grapes. My family has worked the property since then and survived."

"Really?"

She nodded again. Her long curls bounced. Her blue eyes sparkled and a little peach jelly clung to the corner of her mouth. Jared thought she'd never looked more lovely.

"So the Nilsson determination goes way back."

Sassa shrugged. "I guess so. It's taken all the cleverness we have to hang on to our land."

Jared inhaled deeply. "I know the truth of that. When I sold my grandfather's place, I resented the dry dust bowl that sucked so much life out of the man I loved. But now? Now I wish I'd been able to keep the land he'd poured his blood and soul into. I'd have something to show for his years of toil."

Sassa was silent for a moment. Then she reached across the table and grasped his hand. "I think your grandfather would say he has something to show for his hard work."

Jared frowned. "There's nothing left."

"Yes, there is, Jared. You. I think your grandfather would be very proud of who you have become and the work you've done. I know I am. Keri and I wouldn't be here if not for your help."

Those blue eyes and the sincerity of her tone did something to his heart. Discussions about God, confrontation and aspirations disappeared and all he could think about was her deep blue eyes and her inviting pink lips. He leaned forward and touched his mouth to hers. For the second time that morning, his phone rang. Frustrated, he pulled it out of his pocket.

"Yeah?" Jared cleared his throat and tried to sound normal.

Kopack's urgent tone echoed over the cell. "Your drug enforcement team arrived this morning with some new information."

"What makes you so sure it's new? The Spyder compromised the border patrol systems. If my team has the information Chekhov probably has it, too."

"The info comes from a DEA investigation. Their system isn't compromised and your agents had been briefed a while back. We took a chance and contacted the DEA. They're in the thick of their mission and had a new development. They gave us a lead on Rashad Korgay and how he's been shipping the Black Knights' equipment. I think you need to get down here."

Jared rose from the table and walked to the window. "I'm not sure I should leave Sassa." He left out the part about how he'd promised he wouldn't leave her again. Kopack would probably accuse him of being too close to his subject again. The man was right. Jared glanced back at the table where Sassa lifted Keri out of her high chair. Although he wasn't sure "close" was the right word for what was happing between them. He only knew he didn't want to break his promise not to leave her side.

"We have extra men guarding Sassa. Cameras and motion detectors surround her place. She's safer there than anywhere else. I'd like your input."

Pleasure surged through Jared. Sassa's science was beyond his experience. He hadn't been as much help there as he would have liked, but he had become a vital member of the FBI team. That made him feel like a success. It was the kind of feeling he'd been yearning for most of his adult career.

Sassa walked by and placed Keri in the middle of the blanket on the floor. Keri fussed and clung to her mother. But for some reason Jared's feeling of success wasn't as important as the promise he'd made to Sassa. He didn't want to break it.

"I'm still not comfortable leaving her," he said over the phone.

She paused and met his gaze. "Does Kopack need you?"

He nodded.

"Go. Keri and I are fine."

He shook his head but she grasped his arm. "I'm home. I'll be fine."

She wasn't fine. No place was "fine" or safe until the Black Knights were in jail. But if he could help Kopack, it might put them there sooner.

"Where do you want me to meet you?"

"I'll text you the address where the DEA is staging."

Staging? They were planning a major operation. This was serious. Anticipation trickled through his veins. "All right. See you there." He clicked off his phone.

Sassa smiled at him. "I know you promised. I remember. But we really are fine. Like you said, my lab equipment won't arrive until tomorrow and I need the rest. So Keri and I are going to curl up on the couch and wait out this tooth. We're okay."

Still he hesitated.

She pushed him toward the door. "Go. Kopack is waiting."

He snatched his keys from the table and forced himself not to look back.

Jared drove to the address Kopack had given him on the outskirts of Fresno's industrial area. He pulled into the parking lot of a large metal building. He didn't recognize the faded name painted on the side of the building and there were few cars parked in the lot. It didn't look like he was anywhere near a staging area. He left his SUV and headed for the small door at the front of the building. A DEA agent with a bulletproof vest met him at the door.

He was definitely in the right place.

"Are you De Luca?"

"Yeah."

"They're waiting for you at the back."

Inside the empty-looking building was a hub of activity with personnel everywhere. Apparently, it was a command center for a well-established operation. It seemed they transported agents to and from the location so only a few cars parked in the lot.

Kopack stood with several other agents near the center of the massive building. Jared recognized the four men from the border patrol's drug unit. All of them faced the video screen of a surveillance camera. When Kopack saw him, he motioned him forward.

"I think you know agents Crimshaw and Benevetti."

"Yes, good to see you again." Jared shook hands with the two men.

"I'll let Benevetti fill you in."

The agent motioned to the screen. "Two years ago our agents discovered a Mexican drug ring shipping meth lab supplies disguised as auto parts to a location here in Fresno. We let the DEA take the lead. They've had agents working undercover on this project since then. It's been pretty hush-hush. When Kopack told us you were trying to locate a supply route for weapons, we contacted the agents working here."

He nodded to the men working the cameras. "We were fortunate. They had news for us. They were getting close to busting this operation wide open when they discovered a new suspect."

"Who?"

Agent Benevetti pointed to the screen. "See for yourself. He showed up yesterday. We ran a check and it's definitely your man."

On the screen above them was another large metal

manufacturing building. A small door opened and the surveillance camera zoomed in on a man walking out. He wore a baseball cap and sunglasses but he was still recognizable as Rashad Korgay. Jared stepped closer to the computer screen to get a better view. Then he turned back to Kopack.

"Is this live?"

The agent nodded. "We knew he was supplying the Black Knights with their advanced weaponry. We just didn't know how he was getting it into the country so quickly. It was one smart move bringing in your agents. They knew about this operation."

Benevetti took over again. "Yesterday, some very large crates marked 'auto parts' came into this factory building. Korgay arrived with a truck and carted them away. Our men tried to track him but we lost him after an accident at a major intersection."

Jared shook his head. "I doubt that was an accident. The Black Knights work best when they're sacrificing other peoples' lives."

"My thoughts exactly," Kopack interjected. "Today we're set up with satellite tracking. No way is he getting away from us again."

Benevetti agreed. "But we have to move carefully. We can't risk exposing this operation and destroying two years of undercover work."

On the screen, Korgay and another man climbed into a large truck and drove away. The cameras switched to another screen and a view of the truck as it moved out onto a busy road. The truck came to a large intersection.

Benevetti leaned closer. "This is where they lost him yesterday."

The tension in the room was so taut, so heavy, Jared

felt like he could reach out and touch it. As the truck passed through a green light and moved on, relief swept through the group.

One thought ran through Jared's mind as the truck traveled down the road. It was a huge truck. The Black Knights had already made one delivery of this size. What kind of equipment were they transporting? What was the plan?

He moved closer to Kopack. "Do we have any idea what's inside?"

"That's the million-dollar question, isn't it?" The FBI agent exhaled heavily. "They have enough weapons to fight a war."

They exchanged a look. Jared saw his own fear reflected in Kopack's gaze.

Jared spoke slowly. "We need more men."

Kopack nodded. "I've already sent for all the agents Los Angeles and Sacramento can spare. Any more and we'll have to call out the national guard."

Another time Kopack's words would have sounded like a joke. But watching the truck loaded with advanced weaponry move down the road made his words too true.

"What's the plan once we find their location?"

"We'll try to find out how many of the Black Knights are at the spot. See if we can track Chekhov. He's the key."

"I'm not so sure he is the key anymore. His people won't stop even if we capture him."

"You may be right. Let's hope Korgay's leading us to the central location and we can capture them all."

"Chekhov's not that foolish. He'll have his people spread out in different cells and separate locations."

Kopack's small, almost inaudible sigh told Jared the man knew the truth of his statement but was reluctant to admit it. That didn't stop Jared from pushing through the agent's reluctance. "Not to mention yesterday's shipment. They've had twenty-four hours to place those weapons where they want them. We can't sit at that location and watch. We need to move as quickly as Chekhov has."

"I know, De Luca, I know." Kopack's voice was taut. "But I'm losing men, too. I can't afford to rush in and risk more lives."

Another true statement. Jared released a frustrated sigh. They were sandwiched between teetering boulders. One wrong move either way and the Black Knights would discover them.

Kopack turned to him.

Jared could sense the emotions behind the man's tense, knowing gaze. Jared was too emotionally involved with Sassa. His feelings were impeding his duty. Jared looked away unable to deny the truth.

"Why don't you go get a cup of coffee?" Kopack suggested. "I'll call you if there's a change."

Jared nodded. He left the circle of computers and headed to the back of the building where they had created a small refreshment area with drinks, snacks and tables. Several agents sat talking, teasing and laughing. Their normal conversation sent a pulse of remorse through him. Kopack was right. He was too close, bound up in fear for Sassa and Keri, and willing to risk the lives of these men and more like them. They had already put their lives on the line just by being there. They didn't need to take foolish risks. Kopack was right to slow him down. But still… Sassa and Keri were in imminent danger.

He poured himself a cup of coffee but he couldn't sit at the tables. He paced the perimeter of the large building, watching the various agents and officers in their duties.

Two hours passed and he'd made at least ten circuits around the massive building when an agent walked up to him. "Kopack wants you."

Jared dumped the cold, untouched coffee cup in the closest trash container and followed the agent. As soon as he entered the circle, Kopack smiled. "We're fortunate. We followed the truck across town to another building. We accessed videos from nearby security cameras—one benefit of being in a business area is lots of security. We zoomed through the last twenty-four hours of activity at the building."

"Is Chekhov there?"

"No. No sign of him. At least, not in what we've seen. It looks like they broke down yesterday's shipment of goods and sent them out in two other trucks. We've got traces out on those vehicles but nothing so far."

"Then we're no further along than before."

"Yes, we are. We're taking action, De Luca. You were right. Chekhov has his people stationed throughout the city. But we have these Knights…right here. There's been no activity in that building since Korgay's arrival. With five men in the building and a truck full of weapons, we don't need to wait any longer. We're moving now to take them by surprise. Hopefully, we can trace the other vehicles and find the Black Knights location by location. Grab a bulletproof vest and let's go."

The twenty-minute ride across town was the longest Jared had ever experienced. He understood Kopack's strategy to continue putting pressure on the Black Knights. If they kept them on the run, the group would make mistakes and could be tracked down cell by cell. But that would also spread their own men out. With them already stretched thin, fewer people were available if Chekhov made a play to take Sassa. It made Jared feel like the target on Sassa's back just got bigger. He itched to get back to her. He pulled out his phone to call but they'd reached their destination. He shoved his phone back in his pocket.

The manufacturing building where Korgay and the men were hiding was a small, simple metal structure. Bullets would pierce it like an aluminum can. It wouldn't stand up against the barrage about to hit. The men inside would not last long.

Police and government vehicles surrounded the area. Kopack and Jared's vehicle passed a DEA and a SWAT van already in place. Jared couldn't see the teams, but he knew they were there, hidden among the buildings and on the roofs. Just as they stepped out of their vehicle, three well-armed men crept around the corner close to the front of the building. Gunfire erupted. Bullets ripped through the metal structure and pinged off the cars in the parking lot. Jared and Kopack ducked behind their SUV's doors.

When Jared dared to peek over the top, one SWAT team member was being dragged away by his partners. Shaking his head, he sagged to a crouch. So many people injured and dying by the hands of the Black Knights.

Another volley of bullets swept across their SUV. One hit the window of Jared's door and glass shattered down over him. He crawled to the back of the vehicle where Kopack met him.

"What kind of weapons are they using?" Jared asked as another volley of bullets swept overhead.

"I don't know, but the DEA fellows won't wait to find out. The Black Knights might have explosives. We already know they're willing to die. They might blow us up with them. The team has to get in there."

Another barrage of bullets had them both ducking as the SWAT team and DEA agents rallied in a coordinated effort. A storm of bullets zinged back and forth, flying like in a war zone. All Jared and Kopack could do was duck their heads and stay under cover. They didn't have the firepower to contribute.

An engine revved as a small, armored, robotic vehicle plowed across the open area headed for the building. Bullets struck the vehicle and pinged off, but it never stopped. The unmanned vehicle kept on driving forward, straight through the metal wall of the building, breaking through and momentarily exposing the men inside. A new barrage of fire came from the DEA and SWAT snipers stationed on the roofs. Jared saw at least three men inside fall as bullets struck.

The exchange of fire began to fade until all was silent at last. Jared looked at Kopack. He nodded. "Stay here. I'll check with the DEA commander."

Jared eased onto the ground and leaned back against the SUV. His heart was pounding and his mind reeling.

All this firepower focused on one thing…getting Sassa. How could he protect her? He'd need this army of men at the Nilsson house to keep her safe. This whole operation needed to get back there. Now.

He rose from his position on the ground. Apparently,

they'd given the all-clear because Kopack was inside the building. Jared followed him. The SWAT team and FBI agents were examining the bodies and swarming the area but all Jared could see were the massive crates in the middle of the floor, three sealed and three open.

He looked inside the open containers. They were large enough to hold multiple large weapons and all were empty. He found the covers stacked next to the crates with manifest labels stapled to the insides. He recognized none of the names on the manifest except one: EMP. Electromagnetic pulse. A machine to disrupt or destroy all electronic equipment.

It was too high tech, too unbelievable. It made his blood pound. He had to get back to Sassa…now.

Spinning, he searched the area until he found Kopack. The agent had just finished a call when Jared walked up. "Do you see all this equipment? Chekhov is waging war."

Kopack's features were grim. "I see that."

"We've got to get some of these men out to guard Sassa."

Kopack agreed. "First, we've got to mop up this situation and gather as much info from it as we can. Also, the command center just called me. They have a lead on one of the other trucks. If we follow it to another location, we will move quickly. We might just knock the Knights out."

Jared shook his head. "I'm not leaving Sassa out there. I'm heading back."

Kopack tossed him the keys to the SUV. "You go. I'll ride with one of the other units. Keep your phone close."

Jared nodded and hurried back to their damaged but

still functional vehicle. Even after he was on the road, his heart wouldn't stop pounding.

The capture of that building full of supplies should have felt like a victory. But it didn't. Korgay had already made one delivery to Chekhov. The man had advanced weaponry and a small army of people still willing to die for his cause. The FBI was closing the net. Time was running out for Chekhov. But that would only make him more desperate, more willing to risk everything to get his hands on Sassa and Keri.

Jared stepped on the accelerator.

EIGHT

Keri was more fussy than usual. After two days of no sleep, she was beyond the point of no return. All afternoon and most of the evening, Sassa walked the room, bouncing and singing. She'd taken a few moments to light a warm fire as the evening fog rolled in, but that was her only break. Jared hadn't called in hours. Exhausted and worried, she sagged to the couch and pulled her cell phone out to check for a message one more time.

Nothing.

A car pulled into the gravel driveway. She lunged to her feet and hurried toward the door. Jared walked in. He looked as weary and worn as she felt. He dropped his keys and cell phone on the side table. As soon as he saw her, he strode forward, pulled her into his arms and held her close.

He felt so good. His arms made the weary ache in her body fade. The feeling was so strong, it brought tears to her eyes.

I'm only crying because I'm exhausted. It's just a normal reaction.

Don't lie. It feels so good because this is what I've been missing. The perfect partner. The perfect dad. I'm crying because I love him and I know he'll go away when this is all over.

She clung to Jared as those silent arguments raged through her mind. After a long while, she felt the tension in his body. Puzzled, she stepped back. "What is it?"

"It was a rough day. How's Keri?"

"Fussy. When that tooth finally breaks through, she's going to crash. She's been awake all night and day. But I think it's almost over. The tooth is close to the surface."

He nodded but she could see his mind was not on her words.

"Tell me what's wrong. What has you so shaken up?"

He stalked into the living room. "This has to stop, this endless waiting for the Black Knights to do something. We have to take control."

She made a small sound as she settled on the couch, the baby in her arms. "How are we supposed to take control? Chekhov's been one step ahead of us the whole time."

"I don't know. I just know we can't wait here like sitting ducks."

Something had happened, had unnerved him so badly, he didn't even want to tell her about it. "What's wrong, Jared? Tell me what has you so upset."

He shook his head. "All those weapons... Chekhov is gearing up for war."

"What kind of war? What do you mean?"

"He doesn't know you figured out the formula. He still thinks the only copy is Sam's and you're the key to finding it. I can't shake the feeling that he's planning to go all-out to get to you and Keri."

His words chilled Sassa to the bone. Keri began to

fuss and it gave her a chance to clamp down on her sky-rocketing fear. She rose, handed the baby to him and hurried to the kitchen where she washed her hands. When she returned, she began to massage Keri's gums with a soothing natural oil.

"Owww!" Keri chomped down hard on her finger.

"It can't be that bad. She's all gums." Jared's soft tone melted Sassa's heart. If only…

"If only" was a fairytale, especially right now. The Black Knights were determined to see to it that she had no future at all, let alone one with a wonderful husband and a happy child. Fear surged through her again. She lunged to her feet, headed back to the kitchen and grabbed a bottle.

"There's a sharp little tooth in there. It finally broke through." She dropped back down on the couch. "Maybe now she'll rest."

Back in her arms, Keri latched on to the bottle with both hands and began to drink. Apparently, this bout with her first tooth was finally over. But it was the least of their problems.

Clamping on the fear tearing at her insides, Sassa shook her head. "We've tried and tried and still have no idea where Sam hid the formula."

Jared moved to sit on the stone hearth across from her and leaned forward, his elbows on his knees. "Let's start from the beginning. Maybe we missed something earlier…some detail that will make sense now that we have hindsight."

She shrugged. "All right. How far back should we go?"

"Start with the months before the conference. What do you remember?"

Keri settled deeper into her arms. Sassa took a deep breath and closed her eyes. "Sam was spending long hours at home. I picked up more and more of his daily duties at the lab. June was home, too. Sam told me she'd taken a sabbatical from all her volunteer duties. I just thought they were spending much-needed time together."

"June knew he was working on the formula. I think she even might have been assisting him."

"Do you think the Black Knights kidnapped her because they thought she could give it to them?"

"Even if she didn't know the formula, they could still use her to get to Sam. Either way, it was a win/win move for them."

Memories flitted through Sassa and realization filtered through her. "Sam put off answering the conference organizers for months and then…" She paused. "He answered them by phone. Not email. I think he was trying to keep the information from the Black Knights. He knew they had hacked our server."

Jared nodded. "Yes, we advised him to keep off the internet as much as possible. But once he confirmed his appearance, the conference folks posted his name on all the public forums."

"That gave the Black Knights months to plan their attack."

Jared scooted to the edge of the hearth, so close their knees almost touched. "But Sam didn't discover the exact formula for the pathogen until just before he left for the conference. He even talked about cancelling his appearance to keep at his research. But we needed everything to appear normal. We advised him that such a dramatic change in plans might alert the Black Knights.

So he kept up appearances. Then the day before you left for China, he discovered the formula. He refused to use the internet to send it to us. We planned to make the exchange with the man assigned to watch over you, but then Sam refused to make contact."

"The Black Knights told him they had June."

Jared gave a nod of assent. "It was all downhill from there. You and Sam were already in China, a foreign country. We couldn't pull you back without causing a stir. We didn't know if the Black Knights knew about our involvement and we were trying not to alert them. Our efforts were so convoluted and no use at all."

He sighed heavily. "Let's go back to the day you left for China. Did Sam do anything unusual?"

"No. Everything was normal. He followed his usual routine that morning. I even picked him up early enough to stop by the cemetery before we left."

"Wait…you took Sam to the cemetery the day you left?"

"Yes. He visited Christopher's grave every day. Why?"

"Christopher Kruger's headstone bothered me. Did something about it strike you as strange?"

"Only that it was big," she said with a shrug. "Sam was usually so modest and low-key. That huge headstone wasn't his usual style."

"Nothing else?"

Sassa was silent for a moment before surprise filtered through. "The square stones. They're just like the ones on Sam's safe."

Jared nodded. "That's the first thing that struck me. You know how deliberate and meticulous Sam was. I can't help feeling there is some significance in that single line of colored squares. Tell me what Sam did at the cemetery."

"Nothing unusual. I stayed in the car to give him privacy. As far as I could see, he just bowed his head and prayed."

"Did he touch the headstone?"

Sassa tried to visualize that morning in the cemetery and saw the scene clearly. Energy surged through her. "Sam leaned over, placed one hand on top of the gravestone and bowed his head. His raincoat fell open and draped over the side, concealing one hand. He could have touched the stones and I wouldn't have seen it. No one would have seen it. But why would he be so secretive? It was just the two of us."

"There were security cameras in the cemetery. They were having trouble with vandals. Sam knew that and knew he was probably being taped. He wanted to hide his actions."

He paused. "He special-ordered that headstone, Sassa. He could have had a small safe built into it. The headstone is big enough to hold a container."

Realization swept over her like a cold bath. "He wouldn't have needed much space, just room for a thumb drive."

Jared gently gripped her wrist. "And the numbers on the bracelet are the code to open the safe." He twisted the bracelet, careful not to wake an already sleeping Keri.

Sassa stared at the numbers engraved on the plate. When she spoke, her words came out in a whisper. She was afraid to say them out loud. "You were right all along, Jared. It all fits perfectly. Sam *was* purposeful.

He gave me the bracelet so we'd connect the numbers to the safe in his house and the gravestone."

Jared rose and headed to the side table where he'd placed his phone. "We need to alert Kopack to see if he can get a copy of the cemetery's security video. We can see exactly what Sam did that day.

He picked up the cell and made a frustrated sound. "I have a message from him. We must have missed it when Keri was fussing. They've traced one of the Black Knights' vehicles to a location. Kopack and the DEA team are staging another raid."

"What do you mean 'another raid'? Where was the first one?"

He stared off into the distance.

"Jared, what's going on? What are you not telling me?"

He turned and the look in his eyes frightened her.

"What is it? What's wrong?"

"Heiser's dead, but they're still using his tactic. Distract and attack. Like you said, Chekhov's been one step ahead of us. By now he must know that we traced his vehicles to the building where the weapons were hidden. The raid was so big, it's probably all over the news. Chekhov has to know we traced the other truck, too. He probably knows Kopack has a lead on his next location and is on his way." He paused. It appeared his thoughts were churning.

"If Chekhov follows his usual pattern, he'll leave them there, sacrifice his people and use them as decoys. Our forces will be spread out and divided. That will make your location vulnerable."

Suddenly, he lunged toward her. "We have to get out of here. The Black Knights are coming for you."

Sassa's blood pounded through her temples. Jared ran across the room and picked up the radio.

"Lucero? Come in, Lucero. We've got to get Sassa out of here."

The radio crackled. "I just got a report of activity on the—"

The radio went silent. All the lights in the house flashed then went dark. The only sound was the refrigerator cycling down as the power went off completely.

Flickering fire from the fireplace lit Jared's features as he stared at her across the room. Sassa gripped Keri and stood.

"Jared…" Her whispered word died as muffled shots sliced the air.

Jared dared not look at Sassa. If he did, the fear he knew he'd see in her gaze would paralyze him. Right now, he needed to focus, to figure out their next move.

He'd seen the empty container for an EMP at the weapons location. Chekhov had it in his possession and had used it to knock out all their electronics, including the radios and cell phones. Had the agents been able to get word to Kopack before the power loss? Was help on the way? Could they hold on until they arrived?

His mind went over the rooms in the house. Every one of them had large, old-fashioned windows. No room would be safe. Even the bathrooms had large, frosted windows. No place in the house would provide protection from flying bullets.

It was a house made for pleasure, not this kind of madness. Anger surged through him. Chekhov had brought this horror to a place meant for love and fam-

ily. Jared had to find a safe place for Sassa and Keri…
but it didn't look like that was here.

"Do you have a backpack or a baby carrier for Keri?"

"Yes, a front carrier."

"Do you have a flashlight?"

"In the kitchen drawer."

She followed him into the kitchen, where he grabbed
it out of the drawer, turned it on, took Keri from her
arms and handed over the light. "Get the carrier, a jacket
for yourself and a blanket for Keri." She nodded, spun
and ran into the dark, the flashlight's white beam light-
ing her way through the pitch-dark hall.

By the glow of the fire, Jared took out the cartridge
of bullets he'd hidden in the kitchen cabinet. He stuffed
the solid cartridge into his pocket.

Sassa returned with her hands full. She set cotton
balls and tiny earmuffs on the counter before turning
Keri gently in his arms.

"Two days of wakefulness is making her sleep
soundly. I'm hoping these will keep her that way." She
pulled the cotton balls apart and stuffed the tiny pieces
into the baby's ears then placed the muffs over her head.
She leaned into Jared and slid the carrier over the baby's
feet and up her little body. Jared helped as much as he
could. They both held their breath as Keri slipped down
into the sturdy carrier with a bump. The movement
didn't wake the baby. With a sigh of relief, Sassa slipped
a black sweatshirt over her head, lifted the carrier from
his arms and belted the straps around her waist.

"We're ready."

A knock at the door facing the river made them both
jump. Jared pulled out his gun and stepped between Sassa
and the sliding glass of the portal. Agent Lucero's sturdy

frame filled the window. He gestured them forward. Jared hurried to slide it open. Sassa followed close behind.

Even by the dim firelight, Jared could see the mask of worry on the agent's face. His breath came in short puffs from running. "They had some kind of EMP. Everything's dead. The radios…the cars. I got a message out to Kopack before the firing started but…"

Another muffled shot, closer than the others, echoed off to their right. The tall shadows of the eucalyptus trees darkened the area to an impenetrable black blanket.

"They're using silencers," Lucero said without taking his gaze off the trees. "I can't tell how many of the Black Knights are out there. The fog is muffling the sound and confusing the directions, but the gunshots are getting closer. It sounds like they're mowing my men down like grass."

"We can't hold out here. No room is secure."

The agent nodded. "I know. I scouted the house before you arrived."

Sassa grabbed Jared's arm. "We have a boat tied up down at the dock."

Jared shook his head. "The EMP would take out its engine, too."

"We can use the current. There's a bridge about a mile down. We can float to the bridge then climb the bank to the road and flag down help."

Lucero nodded. "Let's go."

Jared pulled Sassa along with him. They hurried outside and he led her down the grassy lawn. Cool mist swept over them and swirled around their feet. The fog muffled their footsteps but cold moisture pierced the mesh of Jared's running shoes, sending shudders up his back.

How could the Black Knights even see to shoot their targets? They must be using some of Korgay's high-tech equipment…and very successfully. They were getting closer and closer.

Sassa ran ahead. Her footsteps echoed on the wooden dock and reverberated through the mist like a megaphone. Jared cringed, wondering how far the sound carried.

The mist over the water cleared. At the end of the dock, the Nilssons' small fishing boat bobbed up and down. Jared grabbed Sassa's arm and helped her step in. Then he began to untie it from the dock.

"Get on board," he whispered to Lucero.

At that moment, gunfire erupted at the back of the house.

Lucero shook his head. "I'll slow them down here."

He ran back up the dock as Jared stepped into the boat. Gunfire flashed in the fog, arcs of red fire in the gray mist. Jared pushed the skiff away from the dock, shoving them into the current. The little boat rocked and spun until the swift current picked them up.

They drifted down river. Mist shrouded the tall eucalyptus trees bordering the Nilsson property. They were surrounded by gray fog. They couldn't see the house or any lights. Soon even the muffled sounds of gunfire stopped.

Sassa caught her breath as the last shot reverberated through the fog. Jared's jaw tightened. They both waited for a long, long while, hoping for more, for any sign that Lucero and the other agents still fought.

But no sound came to reassure them.

After all the muffled gunfire, the night seemed unusually silent. There was no chirp of crickets or frogs, just the shush of the boat gliding through the water.

They reached an area of the river where the fog had cleared. Soon a car engine roared to life. After the deadly quiet, the rumble of the vehicle echoed toward them like the growl of a stalking cat.

Lights flashed in the distance and arced above the water. Suddenly, a car appeared on the dirt road that ran along the bank. Headlights flashed across the grape vineyard to the side. The vehicle moved along the road at a reckless speed, kicking up dust behind its red taillights.

"Get down!" Jared pushed Sassa to the floor of the boat. She clasped a hand to hold Keri's head against her chest then slid to the bottom of the boat.

She gazed up at Jared, her eyes wide and fearful. "Is it following us?"

Jared watched the car bounce over ruts in the road and zip along at a pace not safe for a bumpy road at night. Trepidation filled him as the vehicle disappeared behind a stand of tall cottonwoods. The headlights passed their location on the river then made a sharp turn and disappeared. Jared held his breath, hoping...

The boat floated around a bend. The bridge appeared. On top of it, the car screeched to a stop, headlights flashing along the bridge then turning to shine over the side and down onto the flowing water just ahead of them. The door opened. A figure climbed out, ran to the side and leaned over. The headlights hit Chekhov's white-blond hair as he searched the river below.

"Get up!" Jared reached for Sassa's hand and pulled her to a sitting position. Again, she pressed Keri's head against her chest to keep it from bobbing back and forth. She sat on the seat between them. Jared pulled oars out of the bottom of the boat and dropped them into the water.

Sassa twisted behind her to see the bridge and Chekhov's waiting figure.

"Oh, no," she whispered.

Jared didn't pause to reassure her. He rowed, digging the oars into the dark water. He turned the small boat toward the edge of the river. Another fierce dig of the oars pushed them toward the bank. He rowed with all of his strength, aiming for a tree with branches dragging in the water. Those branches would provide some cover. Two more deep strokes with the oars and the boat skimmed beneath the branches.

"Grab hold!" His voice was low, intense.

Sassa pressed Keri's head to her breast and grasped the branches with her free hand. The current tried to push them farther downriver, but Sassa clung to the branch with fierce strength. Jared dug the oars into the sandy bottom and pushed them close to shore. Once there, he jumped into the icy water. It was so cold it felt like daggers and came up to his knees. He pushed the boat's prow onto the sandy shore.

"Let's go." He lifted Sassa and Keri out of the boat and set them on the bank. They charged up the steep embankment and reached the dirt road. Jared didn't grab the flashlight jammed in Sassa's sweatshirt pocket. He didn't want to give Chekhov any indication of their location. They would make their way by the light of the moon.

But which way would they go?

He couldn't see any lights. Surrounded by dark vineyards and beyond that the darker, taller trees of huge orchards, Jared didn't know where they were or how they might find help.

He took a deep breath and tasted the dust that still flickered in the air from Chekhov's car zooming past. It would only take him seconds to return. Jared's mind stumbled over the thought.

"This way." Sassa grabbed his hand and led him down the narrow path between the grapevines. They'd almost crossed the vineyard when a revving engine sounded behind them. Chekhov had turned the car around and headed back down the road. Straight for them.

"Duck down. He won't see you above the vines."

Jared did as Sassa commanded but it was tough to run and duck his tall figure at the same time. He could barely keep up with her petite form as she dashed through the dirt troughs of the vineyard.

They reached another dusty road they had to cross. They risked exposure in the open space, but it also gave Jared the opportunity to look behind. Chekhov's parked car sat on the other side of the vineyard, its engine running and lights blazing. The door was open and there was no sign of Chekhov. He hadn't even bothered to shut it down before he'd lunged into the vineyard after them.

They had to move faster. Jared dashed across the road and caught up with Sassa. "Do you know where you're going?" His harsh whisper seemed too loud in the silence.

"These are my neighbor's lands. My brother and I used to play here as kids. I know them well. We have to cross two fields to get to their house. We can call for help there."

"Is it far? Chekhov is behind us."

She started to look back but he grabbed her arm and dragged her forward. "Don't stop. Just keep going. I'll worry about him." Nodding, she lunged forward. They'd kept their voices low, mainly for Keri's sake. If she woke and began to cry… Jared didn't want to think about what might happen. Sassa had one hand over the baby's earmuffs, pressing her tiny head against her chest to keep it from bobbing back and forth. Her efforts seemed to be working.

Once they entered the orchard, the taller trees blocked all light from the moon. The sudden shadows forced them to slow. The farther they traveled from the river, the denser the fog became. Twice, Sassa tripped and almost fell. The second time only Jared's timely grab stopped her from tumbling to the ground with the baby in her arms.

He held her back against him. Her breath came ragged and heavy. She trembled so violently, he wondered how she was staying on her feet at all. He wrapped his arm around her waist and held her up, hoping to give her a moment of respite.

"Take deep breaths," he whispered in her ear.

She nodded.

"We need to be careful. If Keri cries, he'll hear her and find us for sure."

She nodded again. Her soft, orange-blossom scent swept over him, making it hard to release her. He gave her waist one last, encouraging squeeze then pushed her forward.

He paused to look behind them.

A branch cracked. He waited, let Sassa move farther

ahead. The mist was swirling. Moving back and forth like a living thing.

Another crackle. Chekhov was close. Jared was sure of it.

He pulled out his gun. Quietly releasing the lock, he aimed and waited. The mist ebbed and flowed.

Suddenly it parted. Chekhov loomed less than thirty feet away. At first he appeared like a headless shadow. His blond hair and features blended into the fog, but his customary black clothing jumped out, making him an easy target.

Jared must have been visible to him, too, because Chekhov halted in his footsteps. His face registered surprise. He swung his gun up.

Jared fired. Chekhov's shoulder jerked. But it didn't stop the man from getting off a shot of his own. A piercing pain shot through Jared's thigh and he tumbled to the ground. He fell sideways and watched as Chekhov retreated into the mist.

Two shots…almost simultaneous. One of them from a gun without a silencer… Jared's gun. Sassa pressed Keri's head tighter to her chest. She stopped running and looked back. Jared lay on the ground. She didn't think or hesitate. She ran to his side.

He struggled to his feet. Even in the shadows she could see the dark stain of blood on his leg.

"What are you doing? Chekhov is right behind me." His pain-filled whisper sounded harsh against the silence.

Sassa looped his arm over her neck and pointed him in a different direction. "Let's go this way."

"Leave me. I'll slow you down too much."

"I'm not going without you, so move!"

He grunted as he took the first step. He didn't make another sound but Sassa felt him tense each time he step-hopped with his wounded leg.

"I got him, Sassa. I got Chekhov." His whisper sounded jagged. "I shot him in the shoulder. It slowed him down but didn't stop him. He's out there somewhere. You have to go on without me."

She shook her head. "There's an abandoned farmhouse on the edge of this orchard. Lars and I used to sneak over there when we were kids. There's a chute leading to the basement. The interior collapsed years ago creating a cubbyhole you can reach from the outside. It's a perfect hiding place."

"All right. Take me there, but then you have to keep going." He stepped wrong on his leg and stifled a cry of pain. She tried to slow down but he hopped on the bad leg and sped up. He made a small grunt of pain each time, but he kept going.

At last the two-story farmhouse came into view. Surrounded by tall eucalyptus, it looked like a normal farm until they drew closer. The wood building was dark with rot, the windows and doors boarded over.

Sassa sighed with relief and carefully hurried around the debris littering the ground near the house. On the opposite side of the building, loose boards covered a shaft. Sassa released Jared. He wavered on his feet but didn't fall.

She pulled and shoved the boards, careful to make as little sound as possible. Steps leading to the basement appeared but were cut off, sealed by a collapsed wall. She pulled more boards away to reveal a hollowed-out space. One corner remained, just enough room for one person.

One person…or one person and a baby.

Sassa knew what she had to do. Chekhov wanted her. She could hide Jared and Keri here and lead that maniac away.

"Come on." She helped Jared ease down. He lay back with a sigh of relief. Carefully unwrapping the blanket from around Keri, she folded it into a pad and pressed it against Jared's wound then pulled his belt loose from around his waist and tightened it around the blanket pad. As she cinched it tight, he closed his eyes and suppressed a groan.

Carefully, so as not to wake Keri, she unhooked the buckles of the carrier.

"What are you doing?" Jared's mutter was jagged.

"It's me Chekhov wants."

Grasping her wrist, he shook his head. "He'll kill us and come after you anyway."

"Not if I lead him away."

"That's crazy. You can't do it."

Sassa carefully lay her daughter in Jared's arms, slipped her sweatshirt off and covered them both with it. Then she leaned forward and kissed him. His lips were cool and felt so wonderful, for a moment she considered staying. She forced herself to push away and cupped his cheek.

"We have no future together, but that doesn't change how I feel about you. I love you, Jared De Luca, and I know you love my daughter. I trust you to take care of her for me."

Jared's lips parted in surprise. "You love me… Wait. You can't leave her. She needs you."

"If I don't escape Chekhov, tell…tell Keri about me. I… I'd like her to see me through your eyes. I'd like that a lot."

He grasped her wrist. "I won't let you do this, Sassa. Don't leave!"

She pulled loose with a jerk. Keri stirred and made a small sound, forcing Jared to quiet the baby or risk giving away their spot. She used his moment of distraction to step away.

"Sassa…" He reached for her again but she avoided his grasp and placed the boards over the hole, covering the two most precious things in her life. Then she ran to the middle of the yard and waited.

Her cheeks were cold. She touched them and found tears running down. Cold skin. Cold night. Cold, hard choices.

In the distance, she heard sirens. Help was on its way. If only she could hold out long enough…

She wiped her tears away. The fog swirled around her. She stood in the middle of the abandoned homestead's clearing. Out in the open, she would make sure Chekhov saw her before she ran. The road was behind her. If she could lead him in that direction, she might reach it first. His injury might slow him long enough for her to flag down help.

She heard a noise and froze. The fog whispered around the trees, amplifying and confusing sound so she wasn't sure where it came from or even what it was. She stood frozen…uncertain.

Then Chekhov marched out from nowhere; his dark clothes parting the gray mist as he came forward. He carried the gun in his left hand. Blood covered his right shoulder and ran down his hand.

Sassa dashed to the edge of the clearing and glanced back. Chekhov followed her, never pausing to search for Jared and Keri. She exhaled in relief.

Thank You, Lord. Take care of them both. I love them so much!

She spun back, turned on the speed and zigzagged through the trees. She had to beat Chekhov to the road. She needed time to wave down a car.

Without Keri's weight to slow her, she ran fast. She was far ahead of Chekhov. She could hear him behind, crashing awkwardly through the leaves and broken branches, not even trying to cover the sounds of his approach. If she paused, she could even hear his uneven breathing. His injury was slowing him down. All she needed to do was to keep ahead of him.

A large branch had broken loose from a tree and covered the path ahead. It blocked her view but she knew the road was just beyond. Exhilaration filled her.

She ran around the branch and charged through the dead leaves…straight into a quarter section of the orchard where all the trees had been felled. Only short stumps remained. She had no cover and was visible to Chekhov…who even now crashed through the branches into the open.

She spun and ran toward the road.

"Stop! Stop there!"

Chekhov's voice was raspy and weak. Too weak. His injury was seriously impairing him.

"Stop or I'll shoot."

She spun around. "You won't kill me. You want the formula."

"No. You're right. I won't shoot you. I'll go back to

that farmhouse where you left your baby and Officer De Luca. I'll shoot them. One bullet for both."

Sassa froze. He was guessing. He didn't know where they were. He'd never find them.

"They're all tucked up, nice and cozy in that corner of the basement."

He knew exactly where they were. He must have seen her coming out of the shaft. Her hopes dropped and her strength sagged. Chekhov had her. Fear froze her legs as he marched across the open space. Closer and closer.

By the silver light of the moon, she studied the face of the man who had murdered her friends and destroyed her life. His skin appeared even more pale and lifeless than that day at the airport when he'd murdered Sam. What was more, he had open wounds on his face and neck. A stench filtered toward her. She winced and turned away.

"Yes. That smell is my flesh, rotting away. See what technology has done for me? I'm the poster child for progress."

"You're the poster child for a psychopath."

"Sassy Sassa. Even now with a gun to your head."

Sassa winced and turned away.

"Yes. I know what Sam called you. We had many conversations, he and I…before he turned against me. I tried to make him understand, tried to show him that what we do will make the world a better place."

"Thousands will die. How will that be better?"

"Some will survive and they will build a better world. They will thank me."

"The world will call you a murderer just like I do."

He looked behind her. She glanced over her shoulder. Headlights flashed down the road, coming their way.

"We're done talking. Cooperate. Take me to where Sam hid the formula or I'll go back to that farmhouse."

"I don't know where he hid it."

He shook his head. "Then you and I will go someplace far away so you can figure out the formula for me. But you have less than two minutes before that car arrives to decide if it's worth your child's life."

She glanced over her shoulder once more. The car was less than a mile away. She needed to get Chekhov away from Keri and Jared.

"All right. Let's go."

He pointed with the gun. "Very wise. Walk to the road."

Sassa turned around and hurried to the side of the paved road. Chekhov moved slower, but when she glanced back, the gun was still pointed toward her. It never wavered.

He stopped and stood slightly behind her and to her right. He held the gun against her back with his left hand and made sure his bloody right hand was in clear view of the approaching vehicle. Then he nudged her into the road. They stepped out. The white truck came to a screeching halt. The headlights blinded them. The door opened and a man jumped out.

"Has there been an accident?" The driver's dark form came toward them. "Should I call an ambulance?"

Chekhov stepped out from behind Sassa and held up his gun. "We'll take the keys to your truck."

The man had stepped into the beam of the headlights. He halted in surprise and slowly raised his hands. "Sure man. Take the truck. Take it all. The keys are inside."

Chekhov raised the gun to aim at the man. Sassa stepped in front of him. "You'll have to shoot me first."

Shaking his head, Chekhov motioned at the truck. "Get in before I'm tempted to go back to that house for the sheer pleasure of destroying you."

Sassa shook her head. "You don't have time to go back. Hear those sirens? They're getting closer as we speak. We need to go now or they'll be on top of you."

He pointed the gun at the white truck. "Go. Get in. You're driving."

She nodded and moved past the man. She met his frightened gaze and whispered, "The abandoned farmhouse. Help them."

The man frowned but gave her a slight nod. Chekhov climbed in the driver's side and slid all the way across. Then he pointed her into the driver's seat. "Climb in."

She stepped in, closed the door and shifted into gear. The owner of the truck was still standing in the middle of the roadway. Chekhov shoved his foot over and stomped on the gas. The truck shot toward the man. Sassa jerked the wheel to the left as the owner of the truck dove to the right. The truck headed for the ditch. For one moment, Sassa considered letting the truck pile into it.

Even though she'd told Chekhov the sirens were close, they sounded too far away and the farmhouse was too close. If they crashed, Chekhov would have time to climb out and go back for Jared and Keri. She gripped the wheel and wrestled the truck back onto the road and jammed on the gas.

In the rearview mirror, she saw blue flashing lights in the sky, still too far away to help. Gripping the wheel, she faced forward.

NINE

Jared wanted to howl. He could have yelled loud enough to shout down the rest of the derelict building. He pushed against the boards, but they didn't budge. The baby stirred in his arms, so he paused and cuddled her close.

In that moment, he heard footsteps. He held his breath. Chekhov was close. He and Keri were easy targets, trapped in this cubbyhole beneath the wood.

He held his breath and prayed. The footsteps passed over them but it was a long while before he released his breath. When he finally exhaled, he dipped his head and pressed his lips to the top of little Keri's head. She was safe but Sassa was out there…facing that madman alone while he…he lay here wounded and aching and helpless. He couldn't think. He couldn't move.

Once again he'd failed.

Jared gritted his teeth to prevent his anguish from slipping past his lips. Pain racked his body and disgust filled his being.

Then the baby shifted and sighed. Her soft breath brushed against his neck. The pulse of that breath was warm and so very light. So very fragile.

Take care of my daughter. Let her see me through your eyes. I'd like that.

Sassa's words reverberated through him. She had entrusted him with the most precious thing in her life. That she would do that astounded him. Humbled him. Left him reeling and shaking.

Sassa loved him. Truly loved him.

He'd been a fool. All the bickering, the snappy comebacks and the put-offs, all of those mechanisms were designed to protect her tender heart. He knew that about her. Understood them and yet he'd failed to comprehend their full meaning.

She loved him.

Yes, she irritated him and constantly challenged him. Yes, she made him face things he'd rather leave buried. But she also showed him how to love deeply, fiercely and unconditionally.

Her confrontational kind of love also helped him heal. Showered in Sassa's love, he'd forgotten Jessica and found deeply hidden memories of his mother. Good memories that would be the tools to help him heal and maybe forgive the woman who bore him.

Sassa had showed him so much and given him everything he needed…and she'd just walked into the hands of a madman while he lay helpless and powerless.

Despair threatened. Made him want to howl again. But Keri stirred in his arms. She sensed her mother's absence. Once again, he marveled at their mother-daughter connection and their unconditional love, yet another important marker in his life. He could have been a part of that…should have been. But now it was too late.

Still, Sassa had left Keri in his care. He couldn't ignore that gift. He had to protect her, had to get her to safety…both of them to safety.

But he was too weak to move. Too light-headed to think clearly.

As he lay helpless and defeated, his grandfather's scriptures came to mind.

Yea, though I walk through the valley of the shadow of death, I will fear no evil: for thou art with me….

God is our refuge and strength, a very present help in trouble…

The name of the Lord is a strong tower; the righteous runneth into it, and is safe…

When work in the fields was tough going on Grandad's aging body, he said those words over and over again…almost sang them in praise. When they watched the news and heard about some tragic event, the scriptures flowed out of his grandfather as if they were a balm that would ease the world's pain. Prayer came to Grandad as easy as his breath. Now they eased out of Jared in the same way.

All along, he'd doubted God's presence in his life and yet the Lord had repeatedly showed him the way, led him to this one woman. This one moment in his life.

The policeman he wanted to emulate. His grandfather who taught him about God and how to love. Jessica who showed him what he didn't want. Even the job he thought as low profile had been a marker, pointing the way. If he had not been at that station in Riverside, he never would have met Sam, never received his message and never met Sassa.

Every moment and every step, God had been leading him to the life He meant him to have…just like his grandfather told him. The scripture was true.

*For I know the thoughts that I think toward you…
thoughts of peace, and not of evil, to give you an expected end.*

An expected end. This was his expected place. The one God had been leading him to, the life Jared had yearned for in his deepest soul…even when he hadn't realized what that life was. But it was slipping through his fingers again.

Where do I go now, Lord? What do I do?

Jared waited in prayerful silence for his answers.

Slowly, he became conscious of sirens close by. So close and loud, Keri stirred.

Were the sirens in answer to his prayers?

Relief swept over Jared…a relief so strong it brought tears to his eyes. More of his granddad's words echoed in his mind.

Sometimes God shows Himself in ways we don't expect.

Jared could add to that now. *And sometimes He shows Himself in the ways He's needed. Thank You, Lord. Thank You.*

Lights flashed through cracks in the boards. Gathering his strength, Jared pushed himself up to his elbow. He couldn't move the boards with any force and hang on to Keri at the same time. He lay her carrier on the wooden step beside him. She stirred again, sensing she was no longer in someone's arms. For the first time that night, her eyes opened. She blinked and puckered.

Jared shoved on the boards but they bounced back into place with a loud crack. Startled, Keri began to cry.

Jared's first impulse was to shush her. Instead, he shoved on the boards again.

"Go ahead, baby. Cry! Cry loud. Let them know we're here."

With strength he didn't have moments ago, he flung the boards back. They flew up and over. Jared sat up. Flashlights bounced over him, blinding him. He raised an arm to shield his face.

"There he is!"

Kopack's voice. Jared sagged with relief then pulled a crying Keri out of the carrier and into his arms.

"Come on, sweetheart. Let's go get Mommy."

Sassa and Chekhov traveled for a long while in silence, putting more miles between the truck and her loved ones. The farther they drove, the better Sassa felt. Still…her mind churned over one thought. When they were safely away, what would she do? She stopped at a main street.

"Turn right," Chekhov commanded. He was going to take her far away, someplace where Jared could not find her.

Should she tell him she had an idea where Sam's formula might be hidden? Would searching for the formula stall him long enough for Kopack and his agents to find Jared and Keri? Then Jared could point them toward the cemetery.

She had no way of knowing how far behind they were. The truck driver's nod assured her he'd understood her whispered directions about Jared's location. Kopack would find him. But would he be conscious and able to tell them where she was headed?

She couldn't put off her decision for much longer.

Besides, a small part of her wanted to know if they

had guessed right. Had Sam hidden the formula in Christopher's headstone?

If the formula was there and she handed it over to Chekhov, he'd have no further use for her. Just like Sam and June, he'd end her life instantly.

Surely, Kopack and the police were not far behind. She'd heard the sirens and seen the lights. Maybe they would come in time.

Or not. Should she risk it?

Her thoughts washed back and forth.

Lord, what do I do?

The freeway on-ramp loomed in front of her. Chekhov ordered her onto it. The headlights of oncoming cars flashed by her with blinding numbness. She waited for the answers to her prayer. But nothing came. No new ideas. No comforting peace.

Miles passed. No new answer would come because she already knew the truth. Had known it from the minute she'd walked away from Jared and Keri at the old farmhouse.

She'd spent her life believing she depended on her loving friends and family to drag her out of her troubles. Then Jared came along and she'd relied on him. That's what she believed, but reality hit her with the force of a slap.

All her loved ones had ever done for her was follow the Golden Rule. "Treat others as you'd like to be treated." They never kept a scorecard of what she owed or asked to be paid back. They never chastised her for depending on them. Those were her words, her thoughts, not theirs.

All they had ever done was love her. But when someone loved her, she began to feel like she "owed" them something. Why?

Because after Erik she didn't trust her judgment with people? Because she didn't want to be hurt again? Or was it because she didn't feel worthy of all the love showered on her?

The truth hit her in a wave. All of her adult life, she'd longed for independence, to stand on her own two feet, but she'd been independent all along. She was strong. She never waited. She made things happen. She confronted.

Jared tried to point that out to her but she'd danced away from the truth. Now, in what might be the last minutes of her life, she had to face it. She'd spent the last few weeks telling Jared how God loved him and yet, all these years, she'd forbidden herself to accept His loving forgiveness.

She had God's forgiveness, she knew that. But she couldn't forgive herself. So she'd hidden her sense of guilt behind a quest for independence.

The truth was, no matter how hard she tried, she'd never achieve that sense of independence because, deep in her heart, she didn't feel she deserved it. If she went on like this, she'd spend her life in an endless quest for something she'd never reach.

She was trapped in her past just as much as Jared.

She should have let go of the guilt, taken a chance on life, accepted the gifts the Lord had given her…forgiveness, a wonderful family and a new love.

But now it was too late.

The numbness cleared. She saw the lights of the city and the signs over the freeway. Clarity came to her and a new resolve filled her. She couldn't give up. She had to get back to Jared and Keri.

Please, Lord, let me live long enough to show him how much I love him...and how much You love me... love both of us.

Chekhov's hand holding the gun had sagged almost to the seat beside her. His head had also drooped. His wound was taking its toll and he was growing weaker.

Slowly, barely moving, she slid her hand along the seat.

"Don't bother. You'll have a bullet in you long before you reach the gun and we would go careening off the freeway. Unless that's your goal—for both of us to end our lives here. I assure you, my followers would carry on my work."

Sassa gripped the wheel with grim reality. More than likely, he'd survive the crash and she wouldn't. Chekhov seemed unstoppable. Bleeding, near death's door, he still managed to intimidate.

A steel core of determination filled her and some of her sass returned. She punched the button to lower the window. "I'm merely trying to breathe. The stench in here is overwhelming."

A wry smile slipped over his lips. "I wear the stench of man's progress, Sassa."

Hearing her name slip off his lips with the sibilance of a snake made her skin crawl.

She straightened in her seat. No way would she allow him to see her fear. He seemed to feed on it. Still...she couldn't find a snappy comeback, but now was not the time for snappy comebacks. Now was the time to act.

She swallowed. "I might have an idea where Sam hid the formula."

"You might have an idea?" He studied her from across the seat before shaking his head. "Your idea is just a stall tactic."

The sign ahead of her pointed the way to the turnoff to the cemetery. She'd almost missed it. Even though Chekhov hadn't yet given her permission, she jerked the steering wheel to the right. The truck screeched across lanes of the freeway. Chekhov hit the door and bounced back...toward her, so close, it startled her. She was late hitting the brakes as they careened down the off-ramp.

Once he righted himself, he raised the gun higher. "You really do intend to die with me, don't you?"

She didn't answer. He was baiting her, trying to get a reaction through intimidation again. She wouldn't allow it to happen. Steel-like resolve filled her. Sam once told her she had laserlike concentration and a will of iron. She needed them both now.

Gripping the wheel, she slammed the brakes hard. With one hand injured and the other holding the gun, Chekhov couldn't break his fall. He slammed against the shoulder belt with a small grunt.

So...he did feel pain. Good to know.

"I'm warning you..."

Sassa ignored him. The light turned green. Two could play at the intimidation game. She jerked the steering wheel sharply and accelerated into the turn, sending him leaning her way again.

When Chekhov righted himself, he placed the gun against her temple.

"One more crazy move like that and my finger might accidentally pull the trigger."

Sassa's jaw tightened. He meant what he said. He was prepared to die, right here, right now.

But the weapon wavered. Even with the muzzle pressed against her temple, his hand trembled. He was growing weaker by the minute. If she could only…

The cemetery loomed ahead. "We're here."

Chekhov made a small sound. "We've searched this place several times and found nothing. You're leading me on a useless chase."

He pressed the gun harder against her temple. The light turned green but she didn't move…dared not move with the gun against her temple and his trembling hand.

She swallowed hard. "This is where I think it might be. If it's here, you'll have no more use for me. If it's not, then I'll drive wherever you want me to go."

For a long while, Chekhov didn't respond. Sassa didn't dare move even with her neck cricked awkwardly to the side. At last the gun drooped…not because Chekhov intended it to move but because his arm sagged. He couldn't keep it stretched out any longer. Sassa closed her eyes and shifted her neck from side to side.

She was right. He was losing blood and growing weaker by the minute. He might not feel much pain but his body was shutting down. If only she could hold out…

"Take me there. If you're lying…" Even his voice was weak.

But she knew what he meant to say. If she was wrong and the formula wasn't in the headstone, it would be the last moment of her life.

Steel will or not, she began to tremble. The light changed to red, giving Sassa a momentary reprieve.

Chekhov raised the weapon one more time. "Are you stalling again?"

She swallowed. "I don't think you want me to attract the attention of the police by running a red light."

Her statement amused him and he chuckled. "I've beat the border patrol and the FBI. The police in this backwater town do not frighten me."

The police in this backwater town are right behind you. I saw the lights of their vehicles.

Finally, a snappy comeback came to her but she dare not speak it out loud. Chekhov was far too unpredictable.

The light changed. She turned right and caught the next green light. All too soon, she was pulling into the drive of the cemetery.

A small, empty gatehouse sat just inside the entrance. She drove past it and the truck parked bedside it. The word Security written in black letters stood out on the white door of the vehicle. Their headlights flashed over the small truck but no one was inside.

Was the driver walking the grounds or asleep on the seat? Had the cemetery canceled the security service? Were the cameras even taping? Did Chekhov know about the cameras?

He had to know about the security. He said his people had searched the cemetery several times. Either Chekhov wasn't worried about the guard or he didn't care about being filmed because he didn't take any preventative measures. Both options meant bad things for Sassa. Still, her gaze shot around the darkened area.

"Don't waste your time looking. The security guards were scheduled to leave the cemetery the day after Sam's funeral."

Sassa's hopes sagged. Did Chekhov and his people know everything? They had been ten steps ahead of them throughout this entire ordeal. How did she hope to gain some kind of advantage now?

She pulled the truck to a stop on the road in front of the Krugers' gravesite.

Away from the streetlights, the fog was thicker. It moved in front of the headlights in wispy waves. Sassa shut down the engine and watched as the lights faded. Moonlight took over and sent a silver glow across the gray marble headstones. Nearby marble statues wavered in the fog and seemed to move.

Sassa shivered. Were these her last moments of life? Here in a cemetery surrounded by shadows and symbols of eternal death?

Images of Jared and Keri crammed into that dark corner of an abandoned basement flashed into her mind. She couldn't leave them. Not like this. She couldn't give up. She had to fight back.

"Let's go." Chekhov had needed time to gather his strength. Now he motioned for her to move. She opened the door and slid out.

"Step back."

He ground out the words. Sassa stepped clear of the door. He had to lower the weapon to pull himself across the seat. He moved so slowly, it might be her chance to run. She glanced around. There was nothing large enough to hide behind. Chekhov would simply raise the gun and shoot her in the back. Now was not the time to make a move.

He slipped out of the truck and his knees buckled. He caught himself only because his gun arm lay across the open window. He lifted himself with sheer willpower, never once taking his gaze off Sassa. He was weak but not so weak he couldn't shoot.

What could she do? Sassa looked at the gravesites. Flowers still surrounded the headstones. A bright blue vase with tall gladiolas stood right in front of Sam's marker. Smaller flower arrangements rested below it and around June's headstone. Christopher's marker was empty.

On the other side of Sam's grave was a large mound of dirt covered by a green tarp. Next to the mound was an empty grave. Ankle-high gold-colored markers surrounded the open pit. Obviously, another funeral service was scheduled for the morning. Would they arrive to find her body in that pit?

Sassa closed her eyes and turned away.

"Show me where Sam hid the formula."

Her eyes flew open. Chekhov came toward her with jerky movements. He was having trouble making his legs work properly.

"Don't worry, Sassa. My trigger finger still works."

She gritted her teeth. He motioned her forward. She turned and headed for the graves. Her back tingled as if a bullet was already screaming toward her. She caught her breath and it came out like a sob.

Help me, Lord. Let me stay strong to the very end. Be with me.

Energy surged through her like electric shocks. Her senses tightened, fine-tuned to a deeper level. The fog brushed against her cheeks like a damp touch. She inhaled the smell of plant decay and the moist, dark dirt of the recently dug grave. Her fingertips tingled with awareness.

Move slow. Take your time.

That was hard to do when her senses were zinging back and forth like electric wires. She headed to Sam's headstone first. She knew the numbers on the bracelet by heart but she twisted her wrist in the light until she could see them. Then she counted each stone out loud for Chekhov and called out the numbers as she pushed the corresponding buttons. Then she waited.

Nothing happened. She looked back at Chekhov. He wavered back and forth like a man about to topple over. But when he saw her looking, he stiffened.

"Clever. Sam was most clever. But you can stop wasting our time. Sam visited Christopher's grave the day before he left. If the formula is anywhere, it will be there."

Sassa swallowed and pushed the tall vase of flowers out of her way. The tips of the soft gladiolas brushed against her fingertips as she stepped across to Christopher's headstone.

The fog drifted over them, obscuring her view. She had to turn in the light to see the numbers. Holding up her wrist, she punched the numbers again and held her breath.

Something clicked. A small V-shaped crescent opened in the headstone. A black thumb drive rested at the bottom of the crescent.

Sassa exhaled a long sigh. Her breath rasped in the cool air.

Chekhov moved up behind her, stumbling as he came forward.

"Is it there?" In his excitement he came closer, close enough for her to reach him. Her senses fired off like snapping electrodes.

His stench hit her again but she refused to back away.

"Give it to me." He held out his hand.

Sassa picked the thumb drive up and gripped it in her hand.

"Give it to me now."

Sassa's fingers clenched around the plastic drive.

"I said give it to me." Chekhov raised his gun.

A flashlight beam hit him in the face. "What's going on here?"

Chekhov jerked his arm up and spun to face the voice behind the flashlight.

Sassa turned, too, her fingers brushing against the tall gladiolas. She gripped the blossoms, crushing the delicate petals, and lifted. The bouquet slid up inside the tall vase. Sassa's breath caught.

Would the flowers come all the way out? At the last minute, the wide stems stuck in the bottleneck but the vase rose off the ground. Sassa swung it around with the full force of her adrenaline-drenched nerves.

The ceramic container struck Chekhov on the side of the head and shattered. He cried out in pain. The gun fired, but his aim went high and wide as he doubled over. Still gripping his head, he stumbled sideways onto the mound of soil beside him. His foot tangled in the green tarp and he fell. He hit his head on the metal barrier around the open grave with a sickening sound. Then he tumbled headfirst into the freshly dug earth.

Sassa ran to the edge of the grave. Chekhov lay at the bottom, his head twisted at an odd angle and his eyes wide open.

The seemingly unstoppable man was dead. Done in by a vase of flowers.

The absurdity of it all hit Sassa and she almost laughed.

"Are you all right?"

The security guard appeared as stunned as Sassa felt. He looked down into the grave and shook his head.

"The police radioed me…said to be on the lookout for you two. I was at the back gate checking the lock when you drove in. They told me just to lie low and observe but then…" He looked at Sassa.

"He raised his gun and pointed it at you. I thought he was going to shoot you." His words stalled.

Sassa gripped his arm. "He was. You saved my life. Thank you."

They young guard's eyes widened even more as shock seemed to overwhelm him. Sassa hugged him and they clung to each other…two strangers in a dark, cold night, fighting shock and glad to be alive.

Police lights flashed over the cemetery. No sirens announced their arrival, but it seemed a hundred white and blue lights filled the dark sky around them.

Lights again. Is that all I'm going to see tonight? Where are the men behind them?

Sassa felt like laughing again. Some part of her knew she was slipping into shock. Her legs trembled. Laughter bubbled up and tears finally fell. Hot, burning rivulets slipped down her cool cheeks.

The cars pulled to a stop. Agents and police tumbled out. Kopack's voice barked orders. She'd never been so happy to hear his brusque tones.

The back door of one police car opened and a tall, familiar form stepped out.

"Sassa!"

Jared limped into the beam of the headlights. Sobbing, she ran forward. He held Keri in one arm and grabbed her with the other. He pulled her so close not even a breath could come between them. She buried her face against his chest and let the tears fall. Then she kissed Keri with wet, sloppy kisses. Her still sleepy baby ducked her head and tried to nuzzle into her mother's neck. Sassa cried even more, amazed that she was alive, that they were safe and that her child was so very comfortable in this man's arms.

Just like her mother.

Jared pressed his lips to the top of her head. Sassa stood on tiptoes, threw her arms around his neck and kissed him with all the love and thankfulness she prayed she'd live long enough to show him.

They stood amid agents and police officers rushing back and forth and barking orders while they clung to each other and kissed. Finally, Jared began to waver. He shuffled Keri into Sassa's arms and stepped back to lean against the fender of the car.

Kopack appeared out of nowhere and grabbed his arm. "Over here!"

As EMTs arrived from the back of the caravan, Kopack met Sassa's startled gaze. "He refused medical attention until we found you. He wouldn't even let the policewoman take the baby."

Only then did Sassa notice the blanket she'd wrapped around his leg was soaked with blood.

"Jared..."

"I'm all right, Sassa. Really..."

He collapsed into Kopack's arms.

TEN

Sassa stopped outside the university's administration building and took a deep breath. She hadn't been back to these offices since her last difficult meeting with Dean Trujillo when he had all but fired her and sent her packing. Sam had overridden the dean then. But Sam was gone now and Sassa was headed to the dean's office, fairly certain that this time he'd make good on his threat.

Since Chekhov's death almost two months ago, she'd spent her days at her parents' house under strict guard while the FBI rounded up the last of the Black Knights. Kopack had insisted that she not leave their protection until all the terrorists were captured. Chekhov's suicidal rampage to find the formula had decimated the groups' numbers. Only a few remained and had to be tracked down, which stalled the FBI's investigation... and Sassa's life.

Restricted to her family's home all that time hadn't been that bad. It had given her a chance to catch her breath, to heal and to figure out her next move.

Every day of the first month she'd spoken to Jared by phone while he recuperated in the hospital. Their phone conversations had felt distant and impersonal. They'd talked about Chekhov, his actions and the Black Knights' final days. But nothing personal. So much hardship and danger lay between them, it seemed they didn't know how to talk to each other without adrenaline pumping through their veins. Sassa had so much to say to him…how she was ready to put guilt behind her. How happy she would be if he could be content in her small town…with her.

But those were things that shouldn't be said over a cell phone. So many unspoken words between them made their conversations strained.

When Jared was released from the hospital, he was immediately called to Sacramento. Then he traveled to Washington. He'd been gone two weeks now and Sassa hadn't heard a word from him. Everything between them seemed unfinished. They had more to say…at least, she had more to say. But as the days passed and Jared's time in Washington extended, she began to think he would never return.

He was where he always wanted to be, in the high-powered position of his dreams. Kopack spoke of Jared in glowing terms to anyone who would listen. Sassa was certain Jared's superiors were taking the agent's recommendations seriously. She began to think Jared would never come back and her words would remain unsaid.

She told herself it was best this way…best in order for her to move on. She owed Jared her life. She wanted to thank him in a more personal way than over the phone. But truthfully, this ending was probably for the best. If he came back, she might cave, might compromise her values and settle for being second place again. She couldn't allow that to happen. She needed to be content with her life and her baby's safety. For her own spiritual growth and happiness, she needed to be content with where she had landed.

When the FBI gave Sassa the all-clear signal, they packed up their equipment and left. The house and property felt empty once they were gone. Agent Lucero and the others had risked their lives to save hers; some had even lost their lives. She owed them much and struggled not to feel the "debt" she always felt when people cared for her. She spent much time in prayer.

Fortunately, her parents returned. The FBI had recommended they extend their stay with her brother while they concluded their mop-up operation. Finally forced to reveal the true situation to her family, Sassa's mother was furious with her for keeping them in the dark about the danger. But, as usual, her father understood her reasons and supported her decision. Once they returned, Sassa spent several days enjoying her mother's pampering attention and her father's solid, dependable presence.

She wasn't ready to return to her own home near the college campus. In fact, she hadn't been able to walk across the grounds just a few moments ago without her gaze constantly searching the area. It would be a long time before she stopped feeling like someone was watching her. Except for her unresolved relationship with Jared and the call from Dean Trujillo, she would have been content to stay secluded in her family home.

The dean's call had caught her off guard. She fully expected this meeting in his office would signal the end of her days at the university. That thought sent panic bolting through her body. The idea of losing her job, of not being independent, poked at the boundaries of her newfound calm. But she refused to give in to the emotion. She'd given her life over to the Lord again and now she clung to His promises. She was capable. She was independent and, most important, she was alive. Her baby and Jared were safe.

God was good. All the time.

She stiffened her spine and marched up the stairs to the dean's office. To her surprise, she was showed straight in to see him.

He stood at his desk, barely glancing up as she entered. "Ah, Sassa. Right on time. Your usual punctual self."

Punctual self. The dean complimented her? This meeting was starting off on a strange note.

His gaze darted down to his desk, fully aware of her surprise. "Well, I'm sure you're eager to get on with your day. I won't hold you any longer. You'll be happy to know your position is secured. We would like you to continue your work in search of a cure for the pathogen."

"Continue my work?"

"Now that you discovered the pathogen, of course we want to see the cure developed."

Sassa shook her head. His use of "we" sounded far too casual. He glossed over it much too quickly.

But he didn't give her the chance to ask any questions. "The grant awarded to Sam was scheduled to end in July, but there's been an extension. We've received additional funding and in view of your recent rediscovery of the formula, the university council feels you should continue your work with the scientists in Washington."

The Washington scientists. Now things were beginning to make sense. The border patrol had provided additional funding and, for some reason, had requested that she continue working with them. The university council must have pressured Trujillo into agreeing.

Oh, how that must have galled him! She studied his downcast features. He wouldn't even meet her gaze.

She took a deep breath, not sure what to say, but she didn't need to fret. Trujillo was anxious to end the interview and left no room for discussion.

He handed her a file. "This is the agreement. Inside you'll find a new contract from the university and, of course, the terms of the grant. I'm sure you're anxious to get started."

Her lips parted. There was nothing else to say. She took the file, mumbled a thank-you and headed out of the office. Walking in a daze, she exited the building. She was ten steps from the building before reality hit and she turned back to stare up at the black windows of Trujillo's office.

She had a contract securing her position. She was in charge of the research program. With numb fingers, she flipped open the file and skimmed the paragraphs. From the gist of what she read, it appeared the border patrol demanded she head up the program or they would take their grant to another university. The grant also secured positions for Matt, Libby and Jacki. Sassa inhaled slowly and raised her gaze to look across the campus at the lab building.

On the path ahead, a tall figure rose from a bench and began to walk toward her, leaning heavily on a cane.

Jared stopped almost five feet away and put both hands on the top of the cane. Classes had just ended.

Students began to stream from the buildings, crossing the quad and swarming around them.

Sassa barely noticed them. All she could see was the healthy, handsome, dark-haired man in front of her. "Hello."

"Hello."

He gestured to the file in her hand. "How do you like your new position?"

She held up the file. "Did you have something to do with this?"

He shrugged. "Maybe. I wrote the report. I'm sure my admiration for you showed through. I couldn't help but write about how brilliant you are, how you're strong and brave and dedicated to your work."

She shook her head. "I... I don't know what to say except thank you."

His smile faded. "You don't need to thank me, Sassa. There wasn't a word in that report that wasn't completely true. What you did was amazing...not just for the department but for the world. Rest assured, if this university didn't want you, many others would. Your future is secure."

"That doesn't matter quite so much to me anymore." She ducked her head. Now was the time to say all those unspoken words. Now, before he went away. She tried to gather her thoughts, but they jumbled in her mind and jammed at her lips.

"I... I wanted to tell you...but I couldn't do it over the phone. I said some pretty strong things about how you were trapped by your past..."

"All of them true."

She studied his face, searching for some sign of resentment or pain. All she saw was a calm acceptance.

"Well, maybe. But I understood you so well because I had the same problem. I was trapped, too, and hiding my guilt behind a need for independence. You helped me to face that. I wanted to tell you...to thank you."

He shook his head. "I had very little to do with it. You were doing what you always do, confronting the truth head-on."

She gave him a slight smile. "Yes, I confront and you aspire." The last word fell to a whisper as her heart dropped to her toes. Now was the time to say it all, to face more truth.

"I'm assuming they're pretty impressed with you. I'm sure you can ask for any position you want now. They'll give you your dream job."

"They did."

His words made her heart fall to the cement beneath her feet.

Here comes his goodbye. The words pounded through her mind so loud, she almost didn't hear his next sentence.

"It's the perfect job. Exactly where I want to be. Right here in Fresno, supervising their top-priority project."

Warm shock swept over her. Not the bone-chilling fearful shock she'd been experiencing since the Black Knights came into her life, but a warm wave of tingling pleasure. It sparkled across her nerve endings.

"That's...that's not what you wanted. It's not your dream job."

A student bumped into her, pushing her closer to Jared. The young woman turned and apologized but Sassa barely heard the words.

Jared smiled and reached for her fingertips. "Like

you, I had a lot to face. Now I know exactly what I want, and I have some pretty high aspirations. I want the girl of my dreams to marry me."

Sassa shook her head. Those were not the words she wanted to hear. "I'm not the girl of your dreams. That's your ex-wife. I'm a real, willful, sometimes snarky woman who makes people feel uncomfortable."

"You're right. You are a real woman, the kind who trusts in the Lord, stands by her man through thick and thin and fights for him. I didn't realize how much I wanted that until I was lying beneath broken boards in a dark hole, watching the only real woman in my life walk away. I prayed and prayed for her to be safe until I could tell her how much I loved her."

"You prayed?" Sassa's words came out in a whisper.

"I did," he said with a nod. "Right after my life flashed before me. I saw how everyone important to me had been guiding me to where I needed to be…just like you said. The policeman who pointed me to law enforcement. My grandfather's faith and the bible verses that gave me— gave both of us—the courage to move beyond our guilt and fears. I knew then how much I was loved and how all those things and people were put in my life to help me in my most desperate moment."

Sassa couldn't think. Jared's wonderful words resonated in her ears, but only three little words seemed to matter.

"You love me?"

"Of course I do."

Still, Sassa couldn't gather her thoughts.

Jared laughed and shook his head. "You're going to make me do this the hard way, crippled leg and all."

He dropped the cane to the ground and bent on his

good knee. The students streaming past them slowed and began to stare.

Sassa's careening sense jolted into place. She reached for his shoulders. "Stand up, Jared. These people are watching."

"Let them. I can't see any job, any future, without you by my side. You make me strong, make me want to be a better man, but still make me feel like I'm all I'll ever need to be right now, right this minute. You bring out the best in me. You love with the strength of a titan, protect like a lioness and...you make beautiful babies. I want more. Will you marry me, Sassy Sassa?"

All of his wonderful words raced through her brain. She almost forgot they stood in view of Dean Trujillo's office window and that he might be watching. She almost forgot the staring students. Her hand crept out and touched Jared's cheek. She ran her fingers along his strong jawline as his wonderful words echoed through her mind.

Strength of a titan...protect like a lioness... You make me want to be a better man... Sassy Sassa.

Her thoughts stopped there. She gave a negative shake of her head. "Only if you promise never to call me Sassy Sassa again."

Jared lunged to his feet and swooped her into his arms. "Not going to happen. I love my brilliant, fierce lioness. I wouldn't change a thing about her."

The minute his lips touched hers, Sassa forgot to argue. She didn't even notice the cheering that erupted around them.

* * * * *

Dear Reader,

I was fortunate enough to grow up in Southern California in what I considered one of its golden ages…the '60s and '70s. The state has probably had many "golden ages" but for me those years were especially great. It was the time of Jan and Dean, the Beach Boys, the Monkees, Walt Disney and a young Kurt Russell—he went to a nearby high school and I dreamed of meeting him at every football game. I never did, of course. I think he was into baseball.

We even had a local television broadcast of a beach party hosted by a radio DJ named the Reale Don Steele and a blond, teenaged bikini beauty named Kam Nelson. I grew up just twenty minutes away, never missed the show and dreamed about joining that party. It was an exciting time and I was right in the middle of the whirlwind.

Even though I lived less than a mile from the beach, every other weekend during the summer months we traveled to California's Central Valley where we waterskied behind flat-bottom boats with engines that roared up and down the King's River. I absolutely loved skimming across the glass-smooth water at a high speed. At night we sat on the sandy banks and looked up at a million stars. The cottonwood branches brushed the river's edge and we inhaled the scent of ripe fruit from the orchards and vineyards around us. My life felt like one grand adventure!

But all things change, including me. I grew up, married and moved away, but those golden times stayed with me. Twenty years later when my daughter moved to the Central Valley, I returned. I found the warm summer nights, the corner fruit stands, the orchards and the vineyards just as I had left them. For a short while, I felt sixteen again, and I knew some day I'd write about the valley.

I added a few terrorists and killers, but I hope reading this book gives you the same sweet escape!

Tanya

SPECIAL EXCERPT FROM

LOVE INSPIRED SUSPENSE
INSPIRATIONAL ROMANCE

A murder that closely resembles a cold case from twenty years ago puts Brooklyn, New York, on edge. Can the K-9 Unit track down the killer or killers?

Read on for a sneak preview of
Copycat Killer *by Laura Scott,*
the first book in the exciting new
True Blue K-9 Unit: Brooklyn series,
available April 2020 from Love Inspired Suspense.

Willow Emery approached her brother and sister-in-law's two-story home in Brooklyn, New York, with a deep sense of foreboding. The white paint on the front door of the yellow-brick building was cracked and peeling, the windows covered with grime. She swallowed hard, hating that her three-year-old niece, Lucy, lived in such deplorable conditions.

Steeling her resolve, she straightened her shoulders. This time, she wouldn't be dissuaded so easily. Her older brother, Alex, and his wife, Debra, had to agree that Lucy deserved better.

Squeak. Squeak. The rusty gate moving in the breeze caused a chill to ripple through her. Why was it open? She hurried forward and her stomach knotted when she found the front door hanging ajar. The tiny hairs on the back of her neck lifted in alarm and a shiver ran down her spine.

Something was wrong. Very wrong.

Thunk. The loud sound startled her. Was that a door closing? Or something worse? Her heart pounded in her chest and her mouth went dry. Following her gut instincts, Willow quickly pushed the front door open and crossed the threshold. Bile rose in her throat as she strained to listen. "Alex? Lucy?"

There was no answer, only the echo of soft hiccuping sobs.

"Lucy!" Reaching the living room, she stumbled to an abrupt halt, her feet seemingly glued to the floor. Lucy was kneeling near her mother, crying. Alex and Debra were lying facedown, unmoving and not breathing, blood seeping out from beneath them.

Were those bullet holes between their shoulder blades? *No! Alex!* A wave of nausea had her placing a hand over her stomach.

Remembering the thud gave her pause. She glanced furtively over her shoulder toward the single bedroom on the main floor. The door was closed. What if the gunman was still here? Waiting? Hiding?

Don't miss
Copycat Killer *by Laura Scott,*
available April 2020 wherever
Love Inspired Suspense *books and ebooks are sold.*

LoveInspired.com

Get 4 FREE REWARDS!

We'll send you 2 FREE Books plus 2 FREE Mystery Gifts.

Love Inspired Suspense books showcase how courage and optimism unite in stories of faith and love in the face of danger.

FREE Value Over $20

LOVE INSPIRED
INSPIRATIONAL ROMANCE

UPLIFTING STORIES OF FAITH, FORGIVENESS AND HOPE.

Join our social communities to connect with other readers who share your love!

Sign up for the Love Inspired newsletter at **LoveInspired.com** to be the first to find out about upcoming titles, special promotions and exclusive content.

CONNECT WITH US AT:

f Facebook.com/LoveInspiredBooks

🐦 Twitter.com/LoveInspiredBks

Facebook.com/groups/HarlequinConnection